The Book of SECRETS

By A. L. Tait

The Ateban Cipher

The Book of Secrets
The Book of Answers

The Mapmaker Chronicles

Race to the End of the World
Prisoner of the Black Hawk
Breath of the Dragon

The Book of SECRETS

AN ATEBAN CIPHER NOVEL

A.L. TAIT

Kane Miller

A DIVISION OF EDC PUBLISHING

First American Edition 2019
Kane Miller, A Division of EDC Publishing

Copyright © A.L. Tait, 2017
First published in Australia and New Zealand in 2017 by Hachette Australia
(an imprint of Hachette Australia Pty Limited), this North American
edition is published by arrangement with Hachette Australia Pty Ltd.

For information contact:
Kane Miller, A Division of EDC Publishing
PO Box 470663
Tulsa, OK 74147-0663
www.kanemiller.com
www.edcpub.com
www.usbornebooksandmore.com

Library of Congress Control Number: 2018942387

Printed and bound in the United States of America

5 6 7 8 9 10

ISBN: 978-1-61067-827-8

Cover design: Kat Godard, DraDog

For all the girls who go where they want, when they want.
Or will, one day.

CHAPTER ONE

Gabe stared in horror at the small book in his hand. The light from the low fire danced across its golden cover, setting off a shower of sparkles from the rainbow of jewels that adorned it. Its beauty was dulled only in one corner, stained by a dark, spreading smudge of blood.

"Take ... it ... to ..." Gabe bent closer to Brother Benedict, trying to hear the elderly monk's gasped instructions.

"Aidan's ..." Brother Benedict wheezed, his eyes closed and his voice a faint whisper. "Hide ... it. They ... must ... not ... have it."

"Aidan?" Gabe repeated, unsure of what he'd heard, alarmed by the old man's pale, clammy face and, even worse, the blood seeping into Brother Benedict's beetling gray eyebrows. "Did you say Aidan? Who did this to you? I need to get you some help!"

Brother Benedict seemed to gather all his strength, lifting his head as he grabbed for Gabe's hand, smearing his skin with the same blood that darkened the book's cover. "Tell no one," the old man said, and there was no hesitation in his fierce whisper, though his eyes were now watery beneath fluttering eyelids. "What lies within must remain safe."

Brother Benedict sank back to the stone floor and Gabe had to lean in closely to hear him continue. "Find . . . Aidan's . . . on the side."

Gabe paused, waiting, in case there was more, but Brother Benedict was still and the silence around them complete.

Shoving the book deep into the pocket of his robe, Gabe grabbed the thin blanket that had been tossed carelessly to the floor beside the bed, throwing it over the old man. His season in the infirmary had taught him that a sick man needed to stay warm, though Gabe wasn't entirely sure if a gaping head wound constituted "sickness."

He stood, wondering what to do. Surely Brother Benedict didn't really mean for Gabe to leave him lying on the floor while Gabe went off in search of . . . Aidan?

But, Gabe thought, looking around, fists clenched at the destruction, he couldn't stay here either. The tiny circular chamber, usually scrupulously tidy, was a mess, with Brother Benedict's few possessions, along with his bedding and even his thin mattress, dumped on the floor.

Benedict must have disturbed a search of his chamber, and the would-be thieves had beaten him as they'd made their escape – not realizing that Benedict had the book on him, secreted in his robe, much as it was now hidden in Gabe's.

But who would have done such a thing to Brother Benedict? Everybody loved the old man. Brother Malachy joked that Benedict had been born in the foundations of the Abbey as the great walls were being raised and he'd never once left the premises.

Gabe liked to think that's why he and Brother Benedict had such a bond. Gabe hadn't been born at the Abbey, but he'd been left on the doorstep soon after his birth, which seemed close enough.

Life within the Abbey walls had always been calm, peaceful, predictable. Surely no one in the community could have done this to Brother Benedict?

Gabe swallowed as he realized that he must have missed the altercation by minutes. Could he have saved the old man from harm? Or would Gabe be lying down there on the floor beside him?

Then Benedict spoke again, his chest heaving with effort. "Aidan's," he said. "On the side. *They must not have it.*"

Gabe dropped to his knees again. "What?" he almost shouted. "Who is Aidan?"

But there was no more.

"Who are *they?*" Gabe whispered, suddenly feeling very alone in the dim room, the book heavy in his pocket.

Every part of him wanted to run away, screaming for help, but Gabe knew in his heart that Brother Benedict wouldn't now be bleeding on the floor were it not for this book. And he wouldn't have asked Gabe to hide it if it wasn't important.

Tell no one.

Gabe couldn't think now about who'd done this terrible thing. He'd do as he'd been brought up to do his whole life – obey instructions.

Gabe slowly got to his feet, creeping towards the still-open door, feeling the weight of the book against his leg. As he tentatively poked his head through the doorway, looking left and right, Gabe realized for the first time that the corridors and halls of Oldham Abbey were dark and full of shadows. Hiding places.

Swallowing hard, he stepped into the hall and, keeping close to the walls, made his way to the Night Stair. Frowning, he stared down into the yawning darkness, realizing that someone had doused all the cresset lights that always burned low to light the way to matins.

Placing a shaking hand on the rail, Gabe began to feel his way down the winding staircase, trying to keep his sandals from slapping against the stone. He could hear his own breath, harsh and ragged, and tried to calm himself. If someone was waiting in the darkness to grab any unsuspecting novice who was passing, it was probably best not to alert them in advance.

A scuttling sound overhead distracted him and Gabe froze, but there was no further noise. An eerie silence had settled over the monastery, almost as though the very stones held their breath. In the fourteen years he'd been at the Abbey, he couldn't remember a time it had ever been so quiet.

Gabe took another step down before freezing again, listening hard, but heard nothing. He waited another moment before gathering up his robe in his free hand so he could move more quickly down the stairs, wincing as a sharp corner of the book connected with his thigh.

Did Brother Benedict really mean for him to keep it buried in his pocket? Surely it would be better to hand it to Prior Dismas, who was second in charge of the Abbey.

Pressing himself against the wall, Gabe continued to creep down the stairs, desperately probing the old man's words for answers. His instructions were clear, but Gabe couldn't understand them at all.

It seemed strange to Gabe that the Brother had chosen this one manuscript from the many he cared for within the walls of the Librarium. Gabe had spent a lot of time in the Librarium with the old man over the years, even before Gabe had done his one prescribed season there to learn the basics of the work, and long after Gabe had decided, two years ago, that he would devote his life to working in the Scriptorium. Brother Benedict had been disappointed, but Gabe knew he wanted to copy and illustrate manuscripts, not to simply catalog and care for them.

But Brother Benedict cared for all of his manuscripts with the same level of devotion. Gabe had never once seen him favor one manuscript over the others. So what made this one so special?

On top of this, he'd never heard of Brother Aidan, and he knew every monk at Oldham. And how was he meant to hide the book from someone if he didn't even know who they were?

Gabe felt close to tears as he wrestled with the questions – as well as with his first instinct, which was to get help for Benedict.

Tell no one. Hide it.

Gabe stopped short, once again torn between doing as he was told and doing what he wanted to do. Surely a quick detour to the Infirmarium wasn't going to make a difference? He wouldn't mention the book, he'd just say that Brother Benedict needed help.

Feeling better now that he'd made a decision, Gabe once again began making his way down the stairs. Reaching the bottom, he ran lightly along the stone corridor, the jeweled cover of the manuscript scraping against his leg even through the thick, felted wool of his robe.

His mouth went dry as he considered the possibility of being caught with the manuscript in his pocket. Would-be thieves or *they* aside, every manuscript in the Librarium was worth a king's ransom and the precious cover of this one must make it even more valuable.

Just having it on his person was an offense, and Gabe had heard tales of people being hanged for less.

Gabe turned right into the cloister, the wide covered walkway around the Abbey's large central quadrangle, which was well lit and always busy, no matter what time of day or night. Gabe deliberately slowed his pace to match that of the hooded Brothers who seemed to glide by, their sandals making no noise, wanting to draw no attention to himself. He knew exactly what Prior Dismas would say if he caught Gabe running in the hallways.

"If you are to join us as a Brother you must prove that you are no longer a barbarian," Prior Dismas would sniff, as he'd sniffed so many times before.

Gabe frowned at the thought, wondering if the Prior would ever forgive him the accident of his birth. It wasn't like foundlings were unheard of at Oldham – Brother Damman was just a few years older than Gabe and nobody seemed to have a problem with the fact that he'd arrived in a basket as a baby.

Then again, thought Gabe suppressing a grin, Damman was so like the Prior that they might be true brothers – the same small eyes, pinched mouths and thinning blond hair. Perhaps that's why both of them were constantly reminding Gabe that his thick brown hair needed cutting.

Eyes on the ground, Gabe made his way around the cloister, cowl pulled up to hide his face. The Infirmarium was in the farthest corner from the Night Stair, tucked away in another tower, as far from the Abbey's permanent community as possible. The Abbey's doors were always open to the sick and the dying, but they were isolated to keep everyone else safe.

Turning left, Gabe passed the narrow hall that led to the Abbot's chamber. He glanced down it, expecting to see only darkness. The Abbot had been taken ill suddenly the day before. Gabe had seen him at matins, at midnight, but he didn't appear for lauds, the morning mass. Prior Dismas had simply announced at breakfast that the Abbot would return when he could.

The long tables had buzzed with speculation about the nature of the illness, but no one had any answers and conversation had soon moved on to crops and horses and other daily matters.

Now Gabe stopped, spotting a thin sliver of light about halfway down the passage. Was the Abbot in his chambers? Gabe felt a surge of relief. Here was help for Benedict, and surely the Abbot was also the best person to take charge of the book? He and Brother Benedict were the oldest of friends and there was no way that the Abbot could be part of the *they* to whom the Brother had referred.

Trying not to hurry, Gabe nonchalantly looked left and right before ducking quickly into the passage, flattening himself against the wall. He counted to ten before he was sure that no one had followed him and then, keeping his back to the wall, crept along the passage towards the faint light, taking care not to knock over an enormous urn of white flowers sticking out slightly from a decorative crevice in the stonework.

He was so excited at the idea of handing over the burden of responsibility – both for Brother Benedict's condition and for the book – that he'd raised his hand to bang on the door before thinking twice. Before he could start hammering, however, the murmur of voices reached his ears.

Lowering his hand, Gabe tried to swallow his disappointment. If the Abbot wasn't alone, Gabe couldn't tell him about the book. He would go back to plan A and go to the Infirmarium first, then come back and tell the Abbot about the book.

Gabe was turning away when his sharp ears caught the name "Benedict," hissed through the door. He stopped, pressing one ear to the keyhole to listen closely. If the Abbot knew about Brother Benedict, then help would already be on its way and Gabe could creep off to his dormitory, hiding the book until he could see the Abbot in the morning.

"_____ lost to _____ find it for Lord _____. D–!"

Gabe blinked at the curse. He'd heard language like that before, of course, mostly during his season in the guesthouse, tending to the needs of weary travelers who bedded down at the Abbey for a few days whilst visiting Rothwell, the walled city in the valley.

"Where is it?" he heard a harsh voice demand, before it dropped back to an indecipherable whisper. Gabe thought he heard the word "Lord" again, and wondered which of the Abbey's noted patrons the speaker was talking about, before heavy boots stomped towards the door.

Drawing back, Gabe looked for somewhere to hide, knowing that being caught out here by the Abbot or, worse, the Prior, would be disastrous. As he ducked back towards the decorative crevice nearby, Gabe wondered who the boots belonged to. No one in the Abbey wore anything but sandals unless they were leaving for an extended period – undertaking a Pilgrimage or heading to the King's castle in Callchester to pay the tithe. But it wasn't the right time of year for either of those things.

Grimacing in the dark as he slid behind the urn, Gabe was aware of time ticking away and Brother Benedict still upstairs, bleeding or worse.

Keeping his head down, he crouched beside the flowers, their sweet, heady perfume entirely at odds with the deep-seated feeling of dread that engulfed him. He heard the thump of boots as they passed in the hall – not just one set, but many – but could not make out the faces of the men who strode by. It took a moment for him to realize that the men had the cowls of their velvet cloaks pulled up high to hide their features and he shrank back even farther. These men did not want to be recognized – what were they doing in the Abbey?

Finally, the clattering of their boots receded into the cloister and he heard them make their way across the central courtyard.

A hush fell upon the passage and Gabe was about to crawl out of his hiding place, hoping this might be his chance to see the Abbot, when the door opened once more. This time he recognized the voice.

"Clean up upstairs," the Prior said.

Gabe frowned again as another voice muttered a response. This one was too low for him to make out.

"Just make it disappear," the Prior said, and Gabe was startled by the menace in his voice.

"And find that book," the Prior added as a Brother, his hood pulled up over his head and face, passed silently by Gabe's hiding place.

Gabe didn't dare move. Surely the book could only be the one that was buried deep in his robe? Did the Prior already know about Brother Benedict? If so, why hadn't he called in Brother Archibold?

Gabe could hear Prior Dismas pulling the Abbot's door shut, fiddling with the key that locked this inner sanctum. Then he made his way past Gabe, his head lowered as though in prayer, his sandals slapping lightly on the flagstones as he walked.

Watching the thin figure retreat down the hall, Gabe shuddered. Prior Dismas had made it clear that Gabe was not one of his favorite people, seeming to go out of his way to upbraid Gabe publicly for the slightest wrongdoing. He was also very handy with the long, thin willow switch he carried tucked into the back of his belt and Gabe had felt its sting on many occasions.

Gabe counted to fifty before retracing his steps back to the cloister and making his way to the Infirmarium, staying close to the stone walls, trying to stick to the shadows. He saw no one on his route and breathed a sigh of relief as he flew up the stairs to the sick room and saw the round figure of Brother Archibold bent low over his desk, a sputtering candle beside him.

"What is it?" the Brother asked, before Gabe could open his mouth. "Are you unwell?"

Gabe shook his head, the kind concern on the Brother's round face nearly bringing him to tears. "Brother Benedict," he gasped.

Archibold simply nodded and busied himself, picking up his bag of herbs and tinctures. It took a few minutes for the Brother to find everything he needed, while Gabe hopped from foot to foot, waiting, but finally they were ready.

"Show me," said Brother Archibold.

CHAPTER TWO

"I don't understand," Gabe said. "He was here."

Brother Archibold peered through the tiny grated window that adorned the door of Brother Benedict's chamber, frowning.

"Well, he's not here now," Archibold huffed, his face red with the effort of having run across the Abbey after Gabe. He turned away and strode towards the stairs. "You waste my time, young Gabriel, and you should know better. I will report this to Prior Dismas in the morning."

"I don't understand," Gabe repeated, but the Brother was gone.

Gabe gripped the bottom of the window and pulled himself up so that he could see through the grate, feet dangling a few inches from the floor. His heart sank all over again as his eyes confirmed the truth – the chamber was clean, tidy and empty.

There was no sign of the pool of blood that Gabe had seen on the flagstones. The bed was neatly made, with the blanket that Gabe had put over Brother Benedict now stretched tightly across the mattress.

And there was no sign of Brother Benedict.

Dropping slowly back to the floor, Gabe tried to think. What had the Prior said? Something about cleaning up upstairs? Surely he was not referring to Brother Benedict? What was happening here?

Deep in panicked thought, it took Gabe a moment to realize that the bells were clanging. Not the usual gentle bong that gathered the community for prayer, not even the musical peal that accompanied a celebration or announcement. No, this was a jumbled jangle, harsh and compelling.

Around Gabe, doors began to open and Brothers appeared in the hallway, looking at each other in consternation.

"What's happening?" asked Brother Gilbert, cleaning his eyeglasses on his robe before propping them on his nose.

"I don't know," Gabe answered, hoping none of the Brothers would ask what he was doing there at that time of night when he should have been tucked up in the dormitory with the others. "I've never heard the bells like that before."

"It's the alarm," said Brother Malachy. "I've heard it only once before, many years ago. It sounds only in times of war or crime."

Gabe sank against the door. The bells must be ringing for Brother Benedict! Surely, then, he'd been wrong about Prior Dismas? If he'd really ordered a "clean up" in Brother Benedict's chamber, he wouldn't ring the bells now to draw attention to it?

"We'd best get down to the chapterhouse," said Gilbert, interrupting Gabe's thoughts. "We'll soon know what's afoot."

"I hope it's a battle," said Brother Malachy, as he set off towards the stairs. "It's been a long time since I've held a sword."

Gabe gulped, taken aback by the note of longing in the silver-haired monk's voice. He knew that Brother Malachy had been a soldier in the King's personal detail for many years before he'd joined the Abbey, so a battle might be well and good for him, but Gabe would prefer not to have to fight anyone. He'd never so much as seen a weapon, let alone held one. There were abbeys, he'd heard, where monks could train as fierce warriors, but Oldham was not one of them.

"Hush now," said Gilbert, nudging Malachy as they made their way down towards the cloister. "You're scaring the boy."

Malachy laughed. "It's just wishful thinking," he said, turning to Gabe. "Don't fret, young Gabe – it's more likely that someone in the guesthouse has stolen an extra honey cake from Brother Anthony's kitchen and we'll all be back in bed, warm as toast, before matins."

As he followed the Brothers down the stairs, trying to ignore the bump of the hidden manuscript against his leg, Gabe said nothing, not wanting to talk about Brother Benedict. Perhaps Brother Malachy was right, but Gabe felt cold with dread about what might come next.

They joined the throng of robed figures flooding towards the chapterhouse, and Gabe noticed several strangers, still in their nightclothes, also being swept along.

"They've emptied the guesthouse as well," said Malachy, sounding surprised. "This *is* serious."

Gabe took his usual place inside the chapterhouse, squeezed into the back row of hard pews with the others who were not yet fully fledged monks. He slid in beside Nicholas, an oblate, who'd been dedicated to the church by his parents when he was but six years old in the hopes that the family would gain favor and fortune.

Unfortunately, Nicholas, who was now fifteen, preferred to spend most of his time in the stables rather than in prayer, so Gabe wasn't too sure how much benefit the family might be receiving.

"Where were you?" Nicholas whispered. He couldn't have failed to notice Gabe's absence in the dormitory because his bed was beside Gabe's.

"I was in the Necessarium," Gabe said, thinking fast – the fewer people who knew about his visit to Brother Benedict, the better. "I must have drunk too much ale at dinner and I am paying the price."

Nicholas nodded, seeming to accept the explanation.

"Brothers," the Prior began, speaking from the pulpit. "A great tragedy has befallen our Abbey."

There was a ripple of consternation that seemed to echo through the great hall, swirling up into the rafters. Gabe's heart sank. Clearly, Brother Benedict had not survived his beating.

"Brother Benedict has betrayed us!" said the Prior, his high voice dripping with scorn.

Gabe gasped, unable to believe his ears. He glanced around, noting the shock on every face nearby, all staring at the Prior with open mouths – except for Brother Archibold, who was looking straight at Gabe. Gabe hurriedly turned his eyes back to the Prior.

"He has slipped beyond our walls with the Abbey's greatest treasure, stolen away in the night."

Gabe frowned, knowing that the Prior had to be lying. Gabe knew there was no way the old man had left the Abbey on his own. Hadn't he last seen him prone on the cold stone floor with a gaping head wound? Hadn't Brother Benedict's chamber been swept clean?

Swallowing hard, Gabe knew that he was witnessing something awful here, but he had no idea what to do about it. Nothing in his many years of education on how to be good had taught him what to do in the face of bald-faced badness.

"That treasure must be recovered at all cost," the Prior was continuing, a small smile playing about his thin lips. "We will first search every inch of the Abbey."

Gabe almost laughed, thinking that surely someone older and wiser would now say something. If Brother Benedict had stolen the treasure and left the Abbey, why would it be here? But nobody else seemed to even be questioning the Prior's words.

"You will not be allowed to return to your beds until we have searched your chambers and dormitories," the Prior continued, and Gabe watched as Damman stepped forward with five other monks beside him.

"Pinch Face's favorites," Nicholas muttered to Gabe, who recognized Brother Brophy, a hulking monk who had little to say for himself, in the group. Gabe frowned at the sight of him, realizing that he may well have been the monk who'd passed Gabe's hiding place near the Abbot's chamber.

"Once we have searched the rooms," the Prior went on as his favorites left the hall, "we will search each of you as you leave the chapterhouse."

"Where's the Abbot?" Brother Malachy shouted. "Why isn't he here?"

Gabe cocked his head, listening for the answer to the question that had been ringing in his own head since he'd first seen the Prior in the Abbot's rooms.

"As I told you, the Abbot is ill," said Prior Dismas, as though speaking to a small child. Gabe glanced under his lashes at Brother Archibold and noted that the lines on his forehead were now furrows. Strange that Gabe had seen no sign of the Abbot in the Infirmarium, but then his visit had been very rushed . . .

"I am in charge of the Abbey at this time," Prior Dismas continued, and Gabe wondered if he was the only one who saw the craftiness in the man's expression.

Nicholas shifted on the hard wooden pew beside Gabe, bumping his leg. "Ow," he said, rubbing his thigh, "what have you got in that robe? Arrows?"

All thoughts of Prior Dismas were gone in an instant. The manuscript! He'd been so focused on his thoughts about Brother Benedict and the Abbot that he'd completely forgotten that he had the book in his pocket. *The treasure.*

"Are you okay?" Nicholas asked, peering at him closely.

"Fine," Gabe managed. "I'm just . . . I'm . . ."

"You're?" Nicholas repeated, as Gabe clutched for words. He had to get out of here before the Prior and his team began searching them all. To be found here, with the manuscript in his pocket. It didn't bear thinking about.

"I'm not feeling well," he muttered to Nicholas. "I –"

"Goodness," said Nicholas, "you really did overdo the ale at dinner."

"I think I'll go to the Necessarium again," said Gabe, standing.

"Where are you going?" the Prior's voice boomed from the pulpit, eyes narrowed as he stared down from on high.

"Er, the Necessarium," Gabe managed, trying to sound like a boy with a pressing need.

"Sit down!" said the Prior. "No one leaves this room."

"I – er, but . . ." Gabe stuttered. He looked around desperately for help.

"Let the boy go," said Brother Malachy. "He's been here longer than you have and I doubt he's ever seen treasure in his life."

Gabe wasn't sure if he imagined the tiny wink that Malachy threw his way, but he carefully schooled his expression into blankness. Gabe had never been so glad that Prior Dismas had always seemed to believe Gabe was slightly dim, as though his foundling status made him somehow *less*.

Prior Dismas looked down his long nose at Malachy, but several other monks, including Brother Archibold, echoed Malachy's words, and so the Prior finally nodded at Gabe. "Very well," he said. "But you have five minutes only. Otherwise I send a search party."

Gabe nodded, gathering his robe around him as he carefully squeezed his way down the pew, past the others, trying to hold the manuscript close to him so that it wouldn't hit anyone on the way out.

Once at the end of the pew, Gabe walked quickly to the door that led to the internal passageway, hearing whispered mutiny behind him. The Brothers were unhappy with the Prior's high-handedness, but were held in check by vows of obedience. Gabe desperately wanted to head out into the cloisters and find a place to hide the manuscript until he could talk to the Abbot about what Benedict had said, but that would rouse the Prior's suspicions.

Instead, Gabe made his way down the hall to the nearest Necessarium, slipping inside and locking the door behind him. He'd seen no one on the way, but he'd also seen no way out.

Now Gabe drew the manuscript from his pocket and, holding his breath against the stench that always rose from the latrine, examined the book closely for the first time since he'd held it in the firelight in Brother Benedict's room.

It was a thick volume, only slightly larger in size than Gabe's hand, and, as he turned it over to read the front, he realized that the stiff gold cover was actually thin metal, hinged at the spine, lavishly inlaid with large stones of every color. There was no title, but it was clearly a manuscript of importance.

Gingerly, Gabe opened the delicate cover to discover only a blank page. He frowned. No scribe would waste precious vellum by leaving a blank page before the book began. He turned another leaf – blank again.

Beginning to wonder if a huge prank was being played on him, Gabe hesitated before turning the next page. This time he was rewarded with a breathtaking image of a beautiful tree. Gabe could almost hear the wind rustling through the leaves, such was the detail in the picture, each leaf depicted in a different shade of green, the trunk strong and brown, the branches wide and sturdy. A thin frame of gold highlighted the illumination, reflecting the only element of the picture that appeared even slightly unnatural – a tiny golden bird perched high in the branches, mouth open, its very expression suggesting it was singing the most glorious melody.

Gabe shook his head in awe. He had been working in the Scriptorium for two years now and could say, with modesty, that he was considered to have a fair hand with an ink brush, but he could not for one moment imagine creating something as magical as this image. He wanted only to sit here and to look upon it, for he could feel that there was much to learn from this picture.

Steeling himself to leave the tree, he turned the page – and stopped.

There was another beautiful botanical illustration, this time a detailed outline of a smaller plant, from root to flower, but it was the words that confused him. The book was written in a jumble of letters and unfamiliar characters, unlike any language he'd ever seen before.

Gabe turned another page, and then another, only to discover more of the same. He flipped to the back of the book, wondering whether there might be some kind of key or coda that explained what he was looking at, but there was nothing. Just three more blank pages.

Staring at the wall, Gabe tried to think. What had Brother Benedict given him? And why must *they* not get their hands on it?

He turned his attention back to the manuscript, aware that the five minutes awarded him by the Prior were well and truly ticking down – and that if he returned to the hall with this book in his pocket it would not only be wrested from him, but that he might very well be handing it over to the "they" Brother Benedict had warned him against.

Gabe was aware that he was dithering again – that's what Brother Benedict had always called it: "dithering." Gabe wished the old man was here right now to tell him what to do, and his stomach sank as he thought of the Brother's empty chamber. He would not see his older friend again in this lifetime, he realized, feeling a hot prickling at the back of his eyes.

Gabe was almost glad when a light rap at the door startled him from his thoughts. And definitely pleased when he recognized the voice that whispered a demand to be let in.

"Brother Malachy?" Gabe asked, relief flooding through him.

"Let me in," the monk whispered again.

Gabe unlatched the door and Malachy slipped inside, bolting it again behind him.

"You've got something, haven't you?" the man said, voice low.

"I –"

"No," Malachy said, holding up his hand. "Don't tell me. If I don't know, I can't tell and you know my vows preclude me from lying."

Gabe nodded. "Brother Benedict gave it to me," was all he said.

Malachy paused and Gabe could almost see his mind whirling behind his impassive expression. "Whatever you have, the Prior wants," Malachy said slowly. "And if the Prior wants it, then I don't want him to have it. I am deeply bothered by the Abbot's absence in all this and as for Brother Benedict stealing away into the night with treasure . . . well, let's just say that I feel our ambitious Prior takes his vow of honesty about as seriously as his vow of poverty."

Gabe couldn't help but grimace. The Prior kept his chamber at the Abbey locked, but this had not stopped the rumors swirling about the thickness of his blankets and the softness of his pillow.

"You will be searched," Brother Malachy muttered, pacing the floor. "Even now, the Prior is watching the door, awaiting your return. He suspects . . ." The older man stopped pacing. "You cannot hide it here," he continued. "This is the first place they'll look." Malachy looked upward, as though searching for inspiration, while Gabe waited.

"You must leave," Malachy finally announced. "Take it – whatever it is – beyond these walls and hide it."

"What? No!" Gabe said, feeling the skin on his arms goose pimple at the idea. "I cannot."

Malachy's intense blue eyes rested on his face. "I know that you've never been outside," said Malachy. "I've argued against that. How can a boy choose this life if he knows no other?"

Gabe barely heard this well-worn argument, which Malachy had been preaching ever since he'd arrived at the Abbey some five years beforehand, worn and gray, looking as though the world had sucked him dry. Gabe had compared his tired face with the calm, rested expressions of the Brothers around him and decided that he never, ever wanted to look that way.

"I like this life," Gabe said now, staring at his feet.

"Only because you know no other," Malachy said, his voice gentle. "But that is not what we are discussing. I am not suggesting you abandon the Abbey forever, simply that you take whatever you have and hide it outside these walls. The woods are dark and deep and the Prior will never find it there."

Gabe wanted to shake his head again, but he could see the logic of Malachy's argument. All he needed to do was to slip outside the Abbey for a few moments, hide the book and then wait until the whole drama blew over. He could then rescue the book and . . .

Who was he kidding?

Malachy's words reverberated through his head: *The woods are dark and deep* . . . Gabe had seen them from the tiny window in his dormitory, a sea of dark-green trees that stretched away on either side of the road to Rothwell. But he'd never been in the woods, or on that road. Gabe had never been outside the Abbey walls. "Maybe you should take it," Gabe blurted, reaching into his pocket as though to draw out the book.

"No!" Malachy hissed, grabbing Gabe's arm. "Do not show me. The Prior has sent me here as the herbalist to fix your ailment – you may thank Nicholas for telling the entire chapterhouse about your overindulgence in ale and Brother Archibold for suggesting that I, and not he, should attend you. This is your one chance, Gabriel. I will return to the hall and announce that you have taken to your bed. The dormitory is sure to have been searched by now, so you will have a small window in which to complete your task."

Unable to believe the speed with which his peaceful life had been turned upside down, Gabe could do nothing but nod mutely in the face of Malachy's certainty. Even now, Malachy was unlatching the door and peering out, head turning this way and that as he searched for danger.

"Right," the older man said, turning back to Gabe. "Go now."

"But —"

A gentle but firm hand took his wrist and pulled him towards the door. "Go now."

Gabe stepped into the hall. He could hear a low murmur from the hall and realized that the Prior must have set the monks to praying.

"I'll be as quick as I can," Gabe said, turning to Brother Malachy, hoping even now that he would change his mind and take on the task himself.

"No more than one hour," warned Malachy, as he too stepped into the hall, pulling the door to the Necessarium behind him.

Gabe gulped as he backed away down the hall. The nearest exit to the outside world was the side door, set in the exterior wall of the chapterhouse.

Every year at midsummer, Gabe had watched from the hallway as petitioners from Rothwell had stepped through that door, bringing alms with which to buy a year of prayer for their family or cause. They presented their alms to the Abbot, along with their request, and he either bestowed the gift of prayer upon them or sent them on their way with a polite thank you, depending on the size of their contribution.

Gabe had always been fascinated by the long line of people who lined up each year, each with a different reason for needing the benevolence of the Abbey. What a sad place the world outside these walls had always seemed to be.

And now he was to step into it.

"Remember," Malachy's voice trailed after him, "one hour. Any longer than that and it won't be worth your life to return."

CHAPTER THREE

Gabe was lost. No, not just lost, but horribly lost. Surely he'd seen this tree with the large hollow at its center before? If not twice before?

Gabe slouched against the rough bark of the tree, willing himself not to cry. He felt as though he'd been walking for days, tripping and stumbling in the dark, the pale moonlight filtering through the dense canopy of trees not enough to light his way.

When he'd managed to get to the alms office without detection, Gabe had been filled with confidence and he'd unlocked and pushed open the heavy side door with enthusiasm. Outside, he'd tiptoed across the dusty road that ran alongside the Abbey walls and slipped into the quiet woods, crouching behind a wide tree to survey the scene behind him and make sure he hadn't been followed.

He'd been surprised to discover that the side door was barely visible from the outside. Inside it was made from timber and painted a deep red. From the outside, however, it had been cleverly disguised with a layer of thin stones stuck on it, blending almost imperceptibly into the stone wall. Perhaps this was to ensure the secrecy of the Abbot's alms chamber, only visible to petitioners when the door was open?

Even at that point, Gabe had been certain it would be just minutes before he found a suitable hiding spot for his burden and could return to the Abbey. But he hadn't reckoned on the maze that awaited inside the forest, where every tree looked the same and paths that seemed visible one moment disappeared behind bobbing branches the next.

Slumping to the ground, his back against the tree, Gabe once again felt the sharp corners of the book press into his thigh. Pulling it roughly from his pocket, he stared at it, wanting nothing more than simply to throw it deep into the trees and be done with it.

It seemed to stare back at him, glinting even in this soft light. Gabe sighed, shoving it back into his robe. Brother Benedict had entrusted the manuscript to him and he would honor his mentor by keeping it safe. As for what it was and as for getting it to "Aidan," whoever he may be, those were problems for another day. Perhaps Brother Malachy could help him to puzzle it all out.

The thought of Brother Malachy brought to mind the older man's words about not being longer than one hour or it would not be worth returning. Gabe frowned. How long had he been out here now?

He got to his feet and turned resolutely in the direction of the Abbey – or at least the direction he *thought* was the Abbey – and began tramping once more through the woods. A soft bed of leaves muffled the slap of his sandals, and Gabe breathed deeply, charmed by the sweet mix of pine, birch and oak that he could smell on the night air. He may not have been into the woods before but, thanks to the efforts of Brother Malachy in the Herbarium and his own work copying out botany manuscripts in the Scriptorium, Gabe could recognize most trees and plants by sight and scent.

An owl screeched nearby, making Gabe freeze, and he watched it fly silently overhead before trudging on.

He was just trying to decide whether or not to climb a tree, thinking that he might be able to see the Abbey from higher up, when he felt a sharp leaf work its way between his foot and the sole of his sandal. Gabe bent down to remove it. His sandals were nothing more than thin leather soles held on his feet with leather thongs – perfect for treading the wide stone halls of the Abbey but, as Gabe was fast discovering, totally unsuited to the rough terrain outside the walls.

Gabe pulled out the leaf and retied the leather thong to tighten the sandals. He was just about to stand up to continue his journey, when a hand clamped over his mouth.

"Don't move a muscle, Sandals," hissed a voice in his ear.

Gabe froze, feeling a sharp point pressing into his ribs through his robe.

"That's it," the voice went on. "Nice and easy does it. Now stand up straight so I can get a look at you."

Gabe slowly stood, aware that the sharpness in his ribs had not moved.

"Well, well, well," said the voice, and Gabe was surprised to realize that it was high and light, like a young boy's. "What have we here? What's a sandal wearer like you doing wandering the woods at night?"

Unable to answer due to the hand over his mouth, Gabe could only try to look sideways at the owner of the voice. He was standing directly behind Gabe's right shoulder, making it impossible for Gabe to see him.

"Eyes straight ahead," the voice said firmly, with an accompanying press with that sharp point into Gabe's ribs, though the hand did shift from his mouth to be placed around his throat.

Gabe stared straight ahead.

"Cat got your tongue?" the voice goaded. "You know it's impolite not to answer a courteous question, don't you?"

"It's also impolite to accost strangers with a sharp weapon," Gabe responded without thinking.

There was a short pause. Gabe had just decided that his impulsive answer was going to get him killed, when he heard a strange snort in the bushes nearby.

"I think Sandals has you there," another voice said.

"Be quiet, Merry," the voice behind Gabe hissed, and he tucked the name away in his mind.

"Quiet, both of you," came a cold voice from above Gabe's head, and he shuddered, realizing that they had him surrounded – and that this voice meant business.

"I think you've proved your point," said a different, piping voice from behind a tree to his left. "You captured him. Now we should let him go and get back."

"Quiet," hissed that overhead voice again. "How many times must I tell you? The less talking the better."

There was a pause, and then the three other voices all whispered contrite apologies.

"Er, I'm lost," Gabe said, taking advantage of the silence that followed and taking heart from the fact that one of them at least wanted to let him go.

"Shut up," said the voice overhead and he heard a scuffling, rustling sound and realized that whoever it was was climbing down to join him and his captor.

"What are you doing out here all by yourself in the big, bad woods, Sandals?" larked the singsong voice in his ear, the hand tightening slightly around his throat. "We don't see your sort out here much."

"Ever," came the cold voice, now just behind Gabe's left shoulder. "Look how young he is. His sort never gets out – they're too worried they'll never go back."

The air around him exploded into laughter, and Gabe was stunned to realize that his captors were . . . giggling.

"Shh," said the cold voice once more. "Search him and then, perhaps, we'll let him go." The last was accompanied by another sharp jab to his ribs, this time on the left side.

Gabe gulped. If they searched him, they'd find the book. There was no way that a bunch of thieves and charlatans (for surely this was what Brother Malachy described when he told his stories of the outside world?) would allow him to leave with his jewel-covered book – and there was no way he could leave without it.

"Oh come on," came the voice Gabe knew as Merry. Gabe thought that this time he detected a yawn. "It's so late. There's no way he's got anything on him – his type never carries anything but a begging bowl."

"I thought this was about practicing," the cold voice said, sounding irritated. "Proving that a *certain member* of this group was up to the task."

"I think I've proved that," said the voice behind his right shoulder, digging that sharp point into Gabe's ribs as though for emphasis.

"Yes, come on, Gwyn," said the voice from the bushes, with another obvious yawn. "Let's go home."

"*I told you, no names,*" hissed the cold voice.

"Yeah, yeah," Merry muttered with another huge yawn and Gabe heard a loud rustling in the bushes, followed by a huge groan. "I'm all tied up in knots down here, can we just go now, please?"

"Oh, all right then," said Gwyn, and Gabe felt a hand press over his eyes. "Come on then, get behind him. You, Sandals, look straight ahead."

Gabe did as he was told and heard more rustling ahead on the left side of the path, followed by the patter of feet. He frowned. These thieves were very light-footed.

"Right," Gwyn continued, removing the hand from Gabe's eyes. "You lot get on home. I'll escort our friend here down the path a bit farther."

Gabe hesitated, not wanting to press his luck, but practicality won out. "Er, could you possibly point me in the direction of Oldham Abbey, please?" he asked.

"What am I, a tour guide now?" Gwyn complained.

"Oh go on," said Merry, and Gabe thought the voice sounded more awake now that it was upright. "Send him on his way."

"Fine," Gwyn ground out before poking Gabe in the ribs again. "Come on, then, move it – we haven't got all night."

As he plodded along, his unseen captor not letting up the pressure on his ribs, Gabe found himself torn between gladness and fear. Half of him was happy that his treasure was still secret. The other half, however, knew that returning to the Abbey, with or without the book, wasn't going to end well for him.

"All right then," Gwyn said, at last. "You keep going straight ahead, turn left at the tall white oak, then right at the birch grove." There was a pause. "You do know an oak from a birch, don't you?"

"Of course!" said Gabe, unaccountably stung. Why it should bother him that a common outlaw would question his intelligence he wasn't sure, but it hurt more than the point in his ribs.

"All right, keep your robe on," said Gwyn. "It's a fair question, given I don't reckon you've ever left the monastery."

"No, I haven't," admitted Gabe. "But we raise seedlings in our Herbarium and have many manuscripts about trees in the Librarium."

"Hmmph," was the response. "Reading about them's not the same as knowing them."

Gabe paused. "Perhaps," he said. "But I can at least tell them apart."

"Stop here," Gwyn said. "This is where I leave you. Do you know 'The Nightingale's Song'?"

"Er, yes?" said Gabe, confused. Why mention a silly children's rhyme now?

"Recite it," said Gwyn, and Gabe felt the pressure leave his ribs at last. "Don't turn around until you do or you'll feel this knife right through to your other side."

Gabe gulped and began to recite:

"Sad and sweet is the nightingale's song,
He sings it 'til the dawn,
A lonely tune that drifts away
And never sees the morn."

As the last word died away, Gabe heard a strange five-note tune whistled deep in the woods behind him, and then silence. He shuddered, horribly aware of being all alone once more, but now even more conscious of the dangers that faced him out here amongst the trees.

Around him, the birds began to sing and Gabe realized that the forest was waking up. He stared up through the canopy of leaves and detected a faint lightening of the sky above him.

He had to get back. Perhaps there was still time to slip unnoticed into his bed before the bells rang for lauds.

He began to run, his spirits rising when he spotted a massive white oak up ahead – surely this was the one the cold-voiced Gwyn had spoken of? As he ran, the book banged against his leg and Gabe realized that he still hadn't found a hiding place for the manuscript. Perhaps the birch grove would present an opportunity? At least he'd be able to find a landmark like that again.

As the white oak loomed closer, Gabe noticed that the path forked around it. Breath coming in gasps, he stopped to lean one hand on its huge, round trunk, trying to still his ragged breathing. As he stood there, he heard voices coming towards him, down the left fork of the path.

Looking around wildly, Gabe threw himself under the nearest bushes, thankful that his brown robe blended in with the dirt. Having encountered one group of cutpurses, he wasn't keen to meet up with another!

"That lily-livered dreamer can't have gotten far. He's scared of his own shadow."

Gabe recognized the rough, terse voice as Damman's, and indignation coursed through his body. He was *not* scared of shadows, his own or anyone else's – after all, look at him here, hiding in the dark by himself. He merely had a healthy respect for the unknown.

"Do you reckon he's got it?" This voice was low, older and unfamiliar. Gabe tried to ease himself farther into the embrace of the bush surrounding him, sliding the manuscript out of his pocket as he did so and pushing it as far as he could behind him, into the thick undergrowth.

"What was that?" The footsteps stopped and Gabe cursed the rustling leaves that had attracted attention. He stilled once more, drawing on a lifetime of prayer to keep his body motionless even as his mind whirled.

"One way to find out," said the older voice, and Gabe heard heavy footsteps approach, thick boots looming into view as he lay, head on the ground. As though in a dream, Gabe watched the right boot shift backward and then thrust forward, kicking out at the leaves just a handspan from his head.

Holding his breath, he tried desperately not to so much as flinch, watching in horror as the boot lifted backward once more, shifting slightly to the left and then . . .

"No, wait!" Gabe shouted, rolling out from under the bush a heartbeat before the boot came forward once again.

"Well, well, well," said Damman, and Gabe looked up from his dust-covered position to see a self-satisfied smirk on the postulant's face. "If it isn't the thief."

"What?" Gabe blustered, coming slowly to his feet and making a meal out of brushing the dust off his robe, desperately trying to think. "I'm no thief."

"That's not what it looks like to me," said Damman. "Nor to my Lord Ronan here."

Gabe looked up into a face that seemed carved from an oak tree, brown, hard and flat, the nose a mere bump on its wide planes. This was a man who'd been in more than one fight in his lifetime.

Close-set dark eyes stared back at him from under soft black curls that were strangely at odds with the rest of the face. Gabe had heard of Ronan of Feldham, Sheriff of Rothwell and Lord Sherborne's right-hand man, but he'd never actually seen him before.

"Search him," was all Ronan said, but Gabe felt the menace in those two words and shivered.

"I was just looking for Brother Benedict," he tried, but Damman grabbed him with rough hands and began patting him down. Gabe could only thank all that was holy that he'd hidden the manuscript. "What are you looking for?" he said, trying to sound innocent. "I have nothing."

"Shut your mouth," said Damman, before standing back with a shake of his head.

"I told you," Gabe said, ignoring Damman and looking only at Ronan.

"What did you do with it?" Ronan demanded, as though Gabe hadn't spoken.

"I don't know what you're talking about," Gabe said, wondering if his face looked as guilty as he felt. He realized that his feet were shifting uneasily in the dirt and consciously stilled them.

Ronan ignored his words once again. "I'll take him to the castle," he told Damman, stepping forward to grab Gabe. "Make him talk."

Gabe swallowed hard as the big hand clenched on his shoulder. The horror stories of those who'd entered Ronan's domain in Lord Sherborne's castle and never been heard of again had filtered through even the strong, high walls of the Abbey.

"Wait! I'll show you," Gabe said nervously, trying to stem his panic. If ever he needed to stay calm, it was now, when he was about to try to pull off the biggest lie of his life – with absolutely no practice in deception. "It's down here."

Gabe wrenched himself free from Ronan, and began walking back down the path on which he'd come. Holding his hands at his side so as not to rub his aching shoulder, he hoped desperately that a solution would present itself as he walked.

Damman and Ronan muttered something to each other, but Gabe didn't look back, willing them to follow him and sighing with relief when he heard Ronan's heavy footsteps on the path.

As the morning sun rose, filtering through the leaves like faerie dust, the only thing Gabe could do was to buy himself time – and pray for a miracle.

CHAPTER FOUR

"I'm definitely sure it was this one," Gabe said in a loud voice.

"Just like you were definitely sure it was the last three," said Damman, frustration making his voice rise. "Enough! This is a wild goose chase."

"I'll decide when enough is enough," said Ronan, and Gabe didn't miss the menace in his voice.

"I'm sorry," Gabe said, trying to be conciliatory whilst his eyes searched the surrounding woods for any hint of escape. "It was dark when I was last here and all the trees look the same."

"Says the boy who topped the class in plant studies," said Damman with a smirk.

"It's different in real life," Gabe said, echoing Gwyn's words. Funny to think that a thief's taunt could help him now.

"That's as may be," said Ronan, "but this is your last chance. If it's not here, it's into the dungeons with you." He hooked his thumbs into his thick black belt as he spoke, drawing Gabe's attention to the stout, polished truncheon that hung from his right hip. His left was adorned with a silver sword.

Gabe's throat was dry as he led the two men off the path, heading towards a large oak tree with a hollow about halfway up its sturdy trunk. "Up there." He pointed, thinking that perhaps he could simply start climbing and not come back down.

"Up you go then," said Ronan, "and no mucking about – I was the castle's champion tree climber in my day and I will follow you up there if I have to."

Cold with fear, Gabe began climbing, knowing that there was nothing in the hollow, not knowing what Ronan would do to him when he learned of this sad truth. The bark was rough under his hands and his feet slipped inside his sandals, but he persisted, knowing he had no choice. He reached a small branch, putting his hand in the V it created where it met the trunk to test its strength. Deciding it was sturdy enough, he dragged himself up high enough to put one foot in the V, before stopping to catch his breath.

"Oi!" came Ronan's rough shout from below. "No dillydallying."

Staring up into the tree above him, Gabe took a moment to take in the beauty of its spreading canopy before resuming his climb. Around him, birds twittered their outrage at his intrusion into their space and he heard scampering paws overhead as a small animal retreated farther up the tree.

Suddenly, furious shouting erupted below. Looking down, Gabe watched openmouthed as Ronan and Damman were lashed together by two smaller figures, who were running around and around the pair with lengths of rope, trussing the men's arms like geese for Christmas.

Red-faced with rage, Ronan rained curses upon the pair, who were implacable in their work, white masks covering their faces, hooded cloaks covering their hair. Then, as Gabe continued to watch, two even smaller figures, also wearing white masks and cloaks, stepped from behind nearby trees and crept up behind the two men.

"Now!" shouted one of the running figures, pulling the rope even tighter on the two men caught in the snare.

With that, one of the figures calmly lifted an arm and brought a large rock down on the back of Damman's head. He stumbled and fell sideways, taking the other man down with him.

The rope bearers stopped and the shorter of the two walked over to place a foot on Ronan's side.

"Hello, Sheriff," came a friendly voice, and Gabe started as he recognized it as one he'd heard earlier that day – Merry's voice, the one from the bushes! "Long time no see!"

"You!" Ronan hissed. "You will rue the day you crossed me."

The masked figure laughed, sounding delighted. "*Again*," it added. "Don't you want to say 'crossed me again'?"

Ronan cursed, an ugly, vicious sound.

"Now, now," said the masked figure. "Manners are everything, Sheriff, and, frankly, I don't think you were showing any to our friend up there. Hence, we simply had to step in."

Gabe felt his face reddening, hearing himself referred to in this way.

"Anyhoo," the masked figure continued, as Damman began to groan, clearly waking up, "we'll be off now. You, Sandals!"

Gabe peered down through the leaves to see that strange white mask looking up at him.

"Come now," said the figure. "We must away!"

"But —"

"What was it the Sheriff here said?" the masked figure asked. "Oh yes, don't dillydally!"

Gabe slithered down the tree, wincing at the splinters piercing his bare legs as his robe rode up.

"Goodness!" came the laughing voice from below. "That's quite a sight from down here."

Gabe felt his face grow hot once again, aware that he wore little under his loose brown robe. In his embarrassment, he let go of the trunk and landed at the base of the tree in an undignified heap. There was a short silence and then the morning air was punctured by great shouts of laughter.

Standing, Gabe dusted off his robe.

"Don't fret, Sandals," said the taller masked figure, standing nearby, still holding one end of the rope. "Skirts are never easy to navigate."

"It's not a skirt!" Gabe refuted hotly. "It's a robe!"

"Whatever you say," came the bored-sounding reply, whilst the other masked figure laughed once more.

"Enough!" came a voice from the trees, and Gabe recognized Gwyn's cold tones. "Grab the boy and let's go! I hear boots down the track."

Listening hard, Gabe could hear nothing but Damman's moans and a breeze dancing through the leaves above, but the two masked figures moved immediately, tying off the rope into a sturdy knot and making for the trees. He paused – perhaps the group that Gwyn heard when no one else did was a group of Brothers, come to rescue him?

"Come on then!" said the shorter one. "Do you *want* to be caught for the third time today?"

Or perhaps not, a quiet voice whispered through his mind, answering his own question.

Hoisting up the hem of his robes and giving the two men on the ground a wide berth, Gabe followed the masked group into the woods, hoping against hope he was doing the right thing.

"What is this place?"

Gabe felt as though he'd been walking for days, stumbling through an endless maze of tree trunks. He'd never realized how beautiful they could be, all crowded together, in shades of cream and beige, tan and chocolate, biscuit and bread crust. He'd also realized that he would never, ever find his way out of here on his own.

Just when he'd thought he couldn't get more tired, they'd pushed their way through a bramble thicket so dense it felt as though the thorns had thorns, before falling – in Gabe's case – into a large, sunny clearing entirely encircled by brambles with a small stream babbling to one side.

At its center was a mighty oak tree as wide as two stable boxes, its heavy branches supported by seven or eight sturdy saplings. The canopy stretched up and over the tree, sagging down to the ground on three sides, with one side cleared.

As Gabe watched in amazement, one of the masked figures approached the trunk and pressed hard on a large knot positioned low on the right – and a small door appeared in the center of this trunk.

"What is this place?" Gabe repeated, in awe.

"This is our home," said the voice Gabe knew as Gwyn, removing the mask and turning to face him, "and if you ever tell anyone about it, we'll string you up and let the foxes have you for dinner."

Gabe's mouth dropped open, but it wasn't the words spoken that held him dumbstruck . . .

"What's the matter?" said the tallest of the thieves, also removing the mask. "Never seen a girl before?"

Gabe's head swiveled between the two of them. One tall and fair with clear blue eyes, her grubby oval face as beautiful as any Madonna painted at the Abbey. The other, Gwyn, the shorter of the two, was also blond, but her hair was closer to white, her eyes pale gray, and the expression on her sharp features was watchful.

"Don't be mean," said another girl, striding towards Gabe. "I'm Merry," she said, shaking his hand firmly, with a wide, friendly smile, and he remembered the yawning voice from beneath the bushes. Gabe took in her twinkling amber eyes, the strength in her handshake and the short cap of red, curly hair that seemed to crackle with energy.

"Good day," he managed politely, reducing her to hoots of laughter.

"Well now, Sandals, I think we've gone beyond social niceties, don't you?" said Merry.

He looked at them uncertainly, noting that the fourth and smallest member of the group had joined them. A small, dark-haired, dark-eyed girl who looked to be about twelve years old, smiled shyly and introduced herself as Midge.

"You're all girls," Gabe said in a daze, regretting the words even as he spoke them.

"What of it?" demanded Gwyn. "You might have noticed we just saved your . . . sandals."

"There's no need to be like that, Gwyn," said Merry, putting a hand on Gwyn's shoulder. "Sandals here is just a bit surprised is all."

Gabe took in the repeated use of "Sandals," and realized he hadn't even introduced himself.

"Gabe," he said. "Gabriel, known as Gabe. I am, I mean. And, thank you – for saving me."

"Pleased to meet you, Gabe," Merry said, seriously. "Now, perhaps you'd like to come inside for a cup of tea and we can talk about why exactly Ronan of Feldham was chasing you up a tree."

"He wasn't –" Gabe began, before realizing that all four girls had disappeared inside the tree trunk, melting away like smoke.

Shaking his head, Gabe could do nothing but follow.

"So this thing that cannot be named is still lying under a bush near the large white oak?" Merry said, stirring her tea and nodding almost imperceptibly at Gwyn, who downed the rest of her own tea in one gulp and slid out through the door, closing it quietly behind her.

"That's right," said Gabe, perched uncomfortably on a wooden crate, still unable to believe he was sitting inside a living tree. The interior space consisted of one large, round room, as tall as two men standing on each other's shoulders. The walls were, to Gabe's surprise, smoothly polished, burnished to a pale toffee color, while the dirt floor was mostly covered by a thick red rug. There was no furniture, bar the wooden crates on which Gabe and the others sat, and he noticed a stack of sleeping rolls lined up neatly against one wall. Above the rolls, a deep shelf had been carved into the tree and on it was what looked like the remnants from a much larger dinner set – blue-and-white porcelain cups and plates.

The only other decoration in the room was a series of wooden knobs that had been fixed into the walls and held weapons – mostly bows of different sizes, leather quivers bristling with arrows, a thick belt with a long knife inserted into a sheath, a tidy crossbow, and an axe dangling from a leather thong tied through its handle.

Gabe sipped his tea, staring wide-eyed at this collection.

"And you cannot return to the Abbey, thanks to your little run-in with, er, Damman, but you say you did not steal the thing that cannot be named?" Merry went on.

Staring down at his bare, dirty feet, Gabe could see the marks where the sandals' straps had been. "That's right," he said.

"So now you must take this thing to Aidan, whoever that might be?" Merry continued.

Gabe nodded.

"I'm not convinced," said the tallest girl, whom Gabe now knew as Scarlett.

Merry laughed. "You never are," she said, and Gabe saw Scarlett's beautiful mouth tighten at the slight. "Nonetheless I tend to agree that we need to know more."

"I don't –" Gabe began. "There's nothing more to tell."

"Where is this Brother Benedict who gave you the thing?" Merry asked and, for the first time, Gabe detected a voice of authority underneath the good humor. He'd thought at first that Scarlett was the leader of this gang of thieves, or even Gwyn with her icy manner, but the more time he spent with them, the more he'd noticed the deference they all gave to the good-natured Merry.

"I told you," he said, "he disappeared."

"And you swear that you had nothing to do with that?" Merry asked.

"Nothing," Gabe said, holding his hands up as though in surrender. "He was my friend . . ." His voice broke on the last word as the events of the turbulent night caught up with him, and his eyes filled with tears. He was tired, filthy and confused. He'd been set upon by thieves, captured by men and dragged through brambles. Worst of all, he suspected that Brother Benedict was dead, and that Prior Dismas knew more about that and the Abbot's disappearance than he should, which meant that Gabe couldn't go home. Ever.

As Gabe rested his head in his hands, he felt a light touch on his shoulder, and looked up into Midge's solemn little face. "It will be okay," she said in her high, lilting voice. "We'll help you – won't we?" These last words were directed to Merry, who sat back on her crate and looked Gabe over.

"Course we will," she said, eventually. "Have we ever knocked back one of your strays, Midge?"

Scarlett muttered something, tossing her long fair braid back over her shoulder and rolling her blue eyes, but Merry and Midge ignored her. Gabe took the opportunity to ask a question of his own.

"How did you find me?" he asked. "You know, to rescue me."

"Oh, we never lost you," said Merry with a grin. "Gwyn kept you in sight, even after she'd left you. And when Ronan showed up, well, she called us all out to help."

Gabe remembered the strange five-note tune he'd heard in the woods.

"I'll tell you what," Merry went on, her gaze fixed on Gabe, who was feeling very, very sleepy all of a sudden. "Why don't you take a moment to have a little rest – you look all done in."

He couldn't answer, as his entire body was engulfed by a huge yawn that seemed to begin in his feet. He suddenly felt overwhelmingly tired, almost falling sideways off his crate. He felt hands grab his shoulders, lowering him to the thick rug, and something soft was shoved under his head. Moments later, he knew no more.

Gabe awoke slowly, gradually aware of the murmur of low voices nearby, his hip digging into the ground, his right ankle weighing heavily on his left. Opening his eyes, he realized that he was alone in a strange room, and it took him a moment to remember where he was – and how he'd gotten there.

Stretching, he got to his feet and crept to the open door, drawn by the voices outside. Peering into the bright sunlight, he saw four figures sitting beneath the canopy of the majestic tree, bent over something that one held in her hands.

"_____ a king's ransom," said Scarlett, and Gabe could hear the awe in her voice.

"_____ Pa," said Gwyn, her strong face twisted with emotion.

Merry replied, but Gabe couldn't catch her words. He craned his neck, trying to get closer whilst staying within the shadows of the room. The movement attracted Midge's glance and Gabe saw her tug Merry's sleeve.

"Ah, Gabriel," the redhead said, turning to face him with her easy smile. "Come and join us. Gwyn has retrieved your, er, 'thing,' and what a 'thing' it is."

"It's not my 'thing,'" said Gabe, walking over to stand beside her, his eyes on the twinkling, sparkling book in her hands, "it belongs to the Abbey."

Merry laughed. "And yet here it is, dropped by you in the middle of the woods."

"I told you," he said, fists clenching, "I'm just keeping it safe."

"I know," she said, and her face softened. "I'm just teasing you. The question is, what do we do with it – and you?"

"You don't have to do anything with me, or it," he said. "I'm going to –"

He broke off. *What was he going to do?*

Merry stood to face him. Gabe noticed for the first time that they were about the same height, but she was brown and strong and he was pale and skinny beside her. She was looking at him with compassion and he shifted uncomfortably before her knowing gaze.

"You need our help," she said, and he couldn't help but nod in response to her straightforward statement. "We are willing to offer it, but there are terms."

Gwyn stepped up beside her and Gabe was struck by the resemblance between the two, only apparent now in the way they held themselves.

"You're sisters?" he blurted.

"We are," said Merry, putting an arm around Gwyn. "Scarlett here is our cousin, Midge is our friend."

"And you live here? All alone?" Gabe gestured towards the tree.

"We do," Merry said. "For more than a year now – well, Gwyn and I for longer. We picked up Midge about a year ago and Scarlett has been with us just a few months."

Gabe looked them all over. They were still dressed as boys, in breeches and tunics with well-worn leather boots. All but Scarlett had cut their hair short – unbraided, hers was now tied roughly at the nape of her neck with a leather thong, a long tail blowing like golden gossamer in the light breeze.

"Why are you on your own?" Gabe persisted, curiosity outweighing social niceties.

Gwyn's face clouded. "That's none of your business," she snapped.

Merry placed a calming hand on her sister's arm, so easily that Gabe knew she'd done it many times before. "Hush, Gwyn," she said. "It's a fair question. Gwyn and I have been on our own since our pa was dragged away by Sheriff Ronan's men –"

"Arrested for a crime he did not commit!" Gwyn interjected fiercely, her hands on her skinny hips.

Merry nodded, turning to her cousin. "Scarlett here decided that she did not wish to marry the old man her father had arranged for her."

Gabe looked at Scarlett's face, which was impassive, though her jaw tightened.

"And Midge . . ." Merry paused, her face softening, "Gwyn and I found her sitting beside the bodies of her parents after some thieves had done their worst."

Gabe gasped but Midge said nothing, only staring up at him with wide brown eyes.

Taking in their stoic expressions, Gabe realized that his cloistered upbringing had shielded him from so much. He shivered. "How do you manage out here on your own?" he asked to break the silence.

Merry's laugh rang around the clearing and the others joined in. "We're not on our own," said Merry. "We're together."

Looking at them all, standing shoulder to shoulder, Gabe felt a brief surge of jealousy. They were so close, so full of life, so . . . free. In the Abbey, Gabe simply did the same thing every day now that he worked in the Scriptorium. He woke, he prayed, he ate, he worked, he prayed, he ate, he worked, he prayed, he ate, he prayed, he slept, he prayed, he slept, and so on to a new day. For a moment he felt dizzy, considering the unstructured life that the girls must lead.

Then he stopped. They might not have his strict routine to contend with, but they were responsible for every meal, every decision, every . . . thing.

"But how do you eat?" he wondered. For Gabe, meals were a high point of each day. He loved turning up to the table, full of anticipation, to discover what the kitchen team had created. The monks ate simple food, as dictated by their vows of poverty, but it was good, fresh food, well prepared, and was one of the reasons that Oldham Abbey attracted so many travelers.

"We cook, silly," said Midge with a gentle smile.

"Midge is a fantastic cook," added Merry. "We've eaten a lot better since she joined us."

"Hmmph," said Gwyn, giving Gabe a fair idea of who had been in charge of cooking before Midge came along.

"My ma taught me," said Midge with a faraway expression, and there was a moment's respectful silence for the girl's lost mother.

"No meat, though," grumbled Gwyn.

Midge fixed her eyes on the other girl. "We don't eat our friends," she said to Gwyn, in a voice that suggested this was an oft-repeated mantra. "And animals are our friends."

"Albert eats his friends," Gwyn countered. "You have no problem with that."

Midge smiled. "Albert has no friends," she said. "Well, none but me, and he hasn't taken a bite out of me."

"*Yet*," muttered Gwyn.

"Er, who's Albert?" asked Gabe, wondering if there was another member of this woodland gang – and whether he should be worried.

"Oh, he'll be here soon," said Midge, squinting up into the sky as though to work out the time from the sun's position. "Not long now."

"Then let's get on with it," Merry said, tapping the book cover. "I want this settled before Albert gets back and Midge gets distracted."

Her smile was infectious, but she was all business and, as the other girls jumped up to gather around her, Gabe could again see the hint of the strength behind her pretty face with its smattering of freckles.

"Oh yes," said Gabe, suddenly nervous again. "The deal."

"Gwyn has come up with a plan to get the Sheriff off your trail, but first we have a question," said Merry.

Looking at Gwyn's expressionless face, Gabe's nerves grew even jumpier. "Er, okay," he said.

"We look at this and see value only in the cover," said Merry. "Lots of value. Is that what you see?"

Gabe stared at them, having never even considered the question. "No," he said, instinctively. "No."

"What is it about? This book?" asked Merry.

"I don't know," he admitted.

"You can read, though, can't you? I thought they taught all you sandal wearers to do that?"

Gabe shifted under Merry's suspicious gaze. "I can," he said. "But not this."

"But why?" asked Scarlett. "I thought once you could read, you could read anything." Gabe did not miss the wistfulness in her tone.

"Well, usually I can," he said. "I read all four of the common languages and copy many more in the Scriptorium. But I've never seen this before."

Merry exchanged a quick glance with Gwyn. "Well, I don't know much about books," she said, "but I know people. And if I know the Sheriff, he's looking to get his hands on this for Lord Sherborne, who will separate the jewels from the gold of this cover, melt it down, and sell it all."

Gabe gasped. "No!" he burst out. "We can't allow him to destroy the book!"

His mind was whirling – surely Prior Dismas had no hand in this? The Abbey's treasures were one of its greatest assets, attracting patrons and visitors, which, in turn, supported the community as it went about its work and its prayer. If word got out that one had been sold or destroyed, the reputation of the entire community was at risk.

Merry nodded, looking satisfied. "Gwyn said you'd say that."

Gabe's eyes flew to Gwyn's face, but the younger girl showed no sign of hearing her sister.

"We've been examining your treasure," Merry went on, shifting the book from hand to hand.

"It's very beautiful," said Scarlett, her eyes shining as enthusiasm overcame her natural reserve. "My father has three books in his library, but they are nothing like this."

Three books, Gabe noted. Scarlett's father was a wealthy man.

"I really liked the pictures of the plants," Midge said, shyly. "I've never seen paintings like that. Someone has looked really hard at the flowers to make them so real."

Gabe considered that they seemed to know more about the book than his cursory examination had shown him, and wondered just how long he'd been asleep.

"I'm not sure if you realized," said Merry, opening the front cover and appearing to tug at the first page and then the last page, "that this gold cover comes off?"

Gabe couldn't contain his gasp of horror as she pulled hard and the shining cover separated from the manuscript. But Merry simply smiled, handing him what was now just a book covered in plain brown leather. Gabe stroked it, feeling how soft and smooth it was, knowing that this was the original cover – and that it was very old.

"How did you know?" he asked.

"Gwyn," Merry said simply. "Gwyn notices the smallest details. Of everything." Merry placed the bejeweled cover in Gabe's other hand before continuing, "So now we have a book and we have a cover. And you must decide which you think is most important."

Gabe swallowed hard, feeling the weight of the gold cover, watching it sparkle in the strong sunlight. He shifted his gaze to the dull, brown leather, admiring the way it contrasted with the gilt-edged pages of the book. He remembered the way his mouth had watered when he'd opened the first page to the illuminated illustration of the tree . . .

A dazzling flash captured his attention, turning it back to the gold cover.

"I don't know," he admitted. In his mind, he could hear Brother Benedict's feeble voice urging him to "take it to Aidan." Did he know the book came apart? Was the manuscript still important without the cover? The cover more valuable with the manuscript? And which of these two things was the Prior *really* looking for?

Gwyn muttered something that Gabe didn't catch, but he suspected wasn't complimentary.

"Trust your gut," Merry urged him. "That's what Pa always said. Your head can be turned, your heart can be wooed, but your gut never lies. What do you feel right down here?" She poked him in the belly.

"Ouch," Gabe said, trying to lighten the mood and buy some time. "I feel sore now."

"Oh, for the love of all things holy," said Gwyn, and stomped away towards the trees.

"Don't mind her," Merry said, patting his arm. "She's got no patience."

"Unless she's stalking something," Midge admonished, checking the sky once more. "Then there's no one better."

Gabe shivered a little at the thought of the keen-eyed Gwyn tracking down her prey. She was smaller than he was, but there was a tightly coiled anger about her that he shrank from.

"Oh, come on," said Scarlett, who was now entertaining herself by creating tiny plaits in the long tail of her hair. "We don't have all day. We've got to put the plan into action."

"You're right," said Merry. She paused, appearing to think. "Let's look at the question another way," she said. "If you had to return one of these items to the Abbey tonight, probably to fall into the meaty hands of Sheriff Ronan, which would you rather it be. Don't think, just hold on to the one that you want to keep and give me the other – right NOW!"

The sudden ferocity in her voice gave her authority and Gabe didn't hesitate, hiding the book behind his back and slapping the gold cover into her hand.

"There now," Merry said, and the smile was back. "See how easy that was?"

As Gabe tucked the book deep into the pocket of his robe once more, welcoming the familiar weight, he couldn't help but think that it was a good thing she turned on her heel in that instant and took the cover over to Gwyn, who was lurking in the shadows of the canopy.

Gabe was still hopping from foot to foot, on the cusp of changing his mind, when a shadow blocked the sun briefly, drawing his eyes upward – just as a large, dark shape hurtled down from the blue towards him. Gabe had a glimpse of brown-and-white speckles atop huge, grasping yellow claws before he threw himself face-first to the ground, hands over his hair, dirt in his nostrils.

A raucous shrieking sound filled his ears and, for a moment, Gabe was afraid it might have been his own screaming. It took him a moment to realize that Midge's voice was providing a soft counterpoint to the earsplitting noise.

Cautiously, Gabe lifted his head, turning it in the direction of Midge's voice. She had her arm stretched out wide and, sitting on her clenched fist, beady eyes focused in Gabe's direction, was a full-sized falcon. A peregrine falcon, if Gabe's eyes didn't deceive him, though how this small girl could possibly afford the most expensive of all hunting birds he couldn't imagine.

"Sorry," she said to Gabe, cheerfully. "He's not fond of strangers."

Gabe got slowly to his feet, still stunned at the sight of the magnificent bird. He'd seen falcons in books, of course – detailed illustrations that showed every detail of the bird's long slate-gray wings, the thin bands of brown and black through the white feathers of its underside, the proud, predatory head and the huge, yellow feet. But he'd never expected to see one in the flesh.

Peregrine falcons were the hunting birds of nobility. The Abbey kept two kestrels and a sparrowhawk, but they were cranky birds – and the falconer, Brother Gilbert, even crankier with any boy who went near them – so Gabe had kept away.

"This is Albert," Midge continued, pulling a small piece of leather from her pocket. "He's been hunting."

She slipped the leather over the bird's head and Gabe saw that it was a hood, which, he knew, falconers used to keep their birds calm.

"You can come and say hello if you like," Midge said.

"No time for that now," said Merry, returning, dusting off her hands, with Gwyn at her heels. "We need to talk about the deal."

Midge nodded, and walked over towards the tree, crooning to Albert as she went.

"O-kay," said Gabe, still startled by the sight of the falcon and wondering what on earth he might have to offer these girls. They'd given him back the book, so they weren't going to steal it. And their plan seemed to involve the cover, so it wasn't that.

"Gwyn is going to help you return the cover to the Abbey," said Merry.

"But –" Gabe blurted in horror.

"Shh," said Scarlett, abandoning her tiny plait to stare at him. "Don't interrupt when Merry is laying out a plan." Her tone spoke of a lesson learned.

"Thank you, Scarlett," said Merry, before turning back to Gabe. "As I was saying – Gwyn will help you get the cover back into the Abbey, where you'll slide it on another manuscript and, hopefully, no one will notice."

Gabe opened his mouth to protest, mind whirling with questions and objections, but Merry plowed on, not allowing him to get a word in.

"If I were you," she continued, "I would take the opportunity to find someone who might be able to shed some light on who this 'Aidan' is."

Gabe began shuffling through possibilities in his mind.

But Merry had not yet finished. "And then," she said, with one of her small, satisfied smirks, "you're going to help us break our pa out of the castle dungeon."

This time, Gabe didn't even try to respond.

CHAPTER FIVE

Where was she? Stumbling along the path, Gabe narrowed his eyes, trying to spot Gwyn in the dark. After spending the afternoon schooling him in the art of breaking into a building, Gwyn had disappeared after dinner, only to re-emerge wearing black breeches and a black tunic. Midge had helped her to rub charcoal through her white hair, dulling it to a dark gray, before Gwyn had rubbed the black muck all over her face as well.

Gabe was to remain in his robe, though his hair, too, had been darkened with charcoal. "It's a shame we can't do anything about those eyes," Gwyn had said, and Gabe had frowned. *What was wrong with his eyes?*

Scarlett caught his confused expression and laughed. "They're a bit . . . memorable," she said. "The color and all."

Gabe had frowned again, shaking his head.

"Don't you know?" Scarlett had asked, surprised. "Haven't you seen them?"

"How would I see my own eyes?" Gabe had responded. "There are no mirrors in the Abbey."

"Reflective glass? Water barrel? Duck pond?" Scarlett had said, with the surety of a beautiful girl who would never miss a glimpse of her own reflection.

"Vanity's a sin," Gabe said, stoutly. *So are lying and stealing*, a voice whispered in his mind, *and you've managed both of those just fine.*

Scarlett giggled. "Wait here," she'd said, skipping from the room, before returning moments later with a small object held in her palm. "Look," she said, thrusting it at him, face out, balanced between her fingers.

Before he could look away, Gabe had caught sight of a pair of green eyes in a pale face. He'd gasped.

"You see," she'd said. "They're the color of grass. I've never seen anything like them before."

Gabe had shut his eyes. "Take it away," he'd said. He'd always known his hair was brown, almost the same as the wool of his robe, but he'd never considered his eye color before. The vivid green with thick dark lashes came as a shock.

In the end, Gwyn had ended the discussion with a simple instruction that he should wear his hood up and not look at anyone directly.

And now here he was, following her into the night whilst the other girls were tucked up in their sleeping rolls in the oak.

"Come on," a low voice urged him from farther down the path. "Not far now. We need to be quick – we've got one chance to do this."

She'd chosen matins as the weakest moment in the daily life at the Abbey. "Two bells past midnight," she'd said. "They're all sleepy and it lasts for ages."

Gabe had no idea how she knew all this, but Merry had not seemed surprised. "Gwyn goes where she likes," was all she'd said when Gabe had questioned her. "Always has."

Watching her now, sprinting lightly through the trees, he wondered if Gwyn was one of those faerie creatures he'd been warned about in his lessons as a child. Gabe knew that many of the villagers who lived within walking distance of the Abbey still believed in faeries and sprites and other magical creatures, despite the best efforts of the Abbey to dissuade them. Gabe had always laughed at the idea of magic, but now he'd met Gwyn he was no longer sure.

She disappeared into a copse of large poplar trees and Gabe hurried to catch up, worried that she'd simply leave him behind in the whispering dark. He'd never before realized just how loud the night was, full of scurrying and rustling, squeaks and shrieks and squawks.

Bursting through the other side of the copse, Gabe breathed a sigh of relief when he saw her, crouched behind a clump of low-growing junipers. Gwyn did not smile as he slid in beside her.

"Must you be so loud?" she whispered.

"I didn't say anything," he said, stung.

"It's not what you say, it's that galumphing noise you make when you walk."

"I do not *galumph*," Gabe spluttered. "I can't help it if my sandals slap the ground – they're not exactly made for hiking."

"Hmmph," Gwyn said. "Well, we're here."

"Where?" he asked.

"The Abbey, of course," she said, parting the leaves in front of them. "Take a look."

To his surprise, Gabe found himself staring *down* upon the Abbey. Gwyn had brought him around the back of the walls, away from the road, onto the small hill that provided a natural windbreak for the community – essential in winter when the storms came roaring through.

"I've never seen it from this angle," he said, looking in wonder at the stone buildings laid out before him, lit from within the walls by the faint glow of torches and candles.

"Yes, well, given you've never left the place before, that's hardly surprising," Gwyn sniffed.

Gabe was about to respond, when the soft ringing of bells drifted up on the night air. "Matins," he said, and for a moment was nearly felled by the longing that surged through him. No matter that he'd grumbled about being woken for matins ever since he'd been deemed old enough to go, now that it was impossible for him to attend, Gabe missed it.

"Time to move," Gwyn said. "You wait here. I'll swing a light when it's all clear."

"How will you –" Gabe began, but she held up a hand to stop him.

"Got the note?" she asked, and he pulled a wafer-thin leaf from his pocket. It had been Scarlett's idea to leave a note under Brother Malachy's pillow, asking about Aidan, along with instructions on how to make contact. Merry suggested the leaf – easily destroyed or discarded – and that Gwyn deliver it.

"Read it to me," Gwyn said now.

"Benedict seeks Aidan. Leave reply with Borlan."

She nodded. "And you're sure he'll know that Borlan is a horse?"

After much discussion, they'd decided that the safest place for Gwyn to visit regularly was the stables, which were situated as far as possible from the Abbot's wing, where Prior Dismas was most often found.

Borlan was Nicholas's favorite horse, and thus the only name that Gabe knew. He hoped that his message didn't prove too oblique for Brother Malachy, but he also didn't want to give anything away should the note fall into the wrong hands.

"I –" Gabe began, wanting to talk to someone about his fears, but Gwyn was gone and, try as he might, Gabe couldn't even see her in the dark. He'd given her detailed directions to Brother Malachy's chamber and she'd seemed to follow easily, suggesting familiarity with the entire Abbey. Just how often had she been behind the walls?

As the silence settled around him, Gabe could feel himself sweating, despite the cool of the night. Feeling for the umpteenth time that the cover was still in his pocket, Gabe ran through his instructions in his head. Gwyn would let him in and then, as she put it, "do some business" whilst he crept to the library, slipped the cover on a suitable manuscript and left, all without running into anyone.

Simple, Gwyn had said.

Perhaps if you were part wraith, Gabe thought now, his mouth dropping open as an arm swinging a lantern suddenly appeared through a now-open door.

Gabe made his way as quickly as possible down the hill, sliding in some loose gravel and no doubt "galumphing," his mouth dry and his heart beating fast.

By the time he reached the door, Gwyn had gone, and Gabe was left to wonder whether he should leave it open behind him, or close it.

Precious moments were lost before he decided to pull it gently to, without fixing the bolt. And then he was off, tiptoeing through the silent halls and passages, making his way to the Librarium.

Gabe reached the cloister without seeing another soul, and could hear the rise and fall of chanting voices from the chapel. He slid behind a column and scanned the great courtyard. The quickest route from here to the Librarium was to go directly across the quadrangle and up the northern staircase to the turret, which meant stepping out into the moonlight, with no chance for cover.

Seeing no one, Gabe pulled his hood up over his darkened hair, tilted his face towards the ground, and strode across the courtyard, trying to look as though he was on a mission from the Abbot.

The Abbot! Even as Gabe walked he decided he would make one tiny detour on the way out – to the Infirmarium to see once and for all if the Abbot was there.

Nobody stopped him and, as Gabe reached the other side of the courtyard, he broke into a run and raced up the stairs, not stopping until he reached the quiet sanctuary of the Librarium. Closing the door gently behind him, he breathed deeply. He'd always loved this room. Its circular shape and deep, wide windows allowed for a sense of infinite possibilities, and he'd spent many hours here, reading as many manuscripts as Brother Benedict would let him.

It was darker in here than Gabe had hoped, the moonlight from outside not penetrating to the center of the room where the books were kept, away from the harm Brother Benedict had told him that light could cause them. Gabe didn't want to use a lantern in case it drew attention. Instead, he went to the shelves, squinting in the gloom, feeling his way along to find a manuscript of the right size.

About halfway along the second shelf he tried, Gabe found a likely candidate. He didn't even look to see what it was, simply pulled the gold cover from his pocket and inserted it into place around the text.

As he slid it back onto the shelf, Gabe knew that no one would be fooled for an instant into believing they'd missed such an item in their first search – the gold cover gleamed amongst the plain browns and greens of the other books. But, hopefully, with the cover back in their hands, nobody would go looking for the rest.

Satisfied, Gabe patted the golden spine, knowing he'd never again touch anything as valuable, before striding back to the door.

Opening it, Gabe looked down the staircase, listening for footsteps. Nothing. Buoyed by his success so far, he flew down the stairs, checked the courtyard, saw nothing and sprinted across. Pausing in the shadows, he noted that the soft chanting had continued.

Now was his chance. Turning left into the dark hall, away from the back door and Gwyn, he tiptoed his way to the Infirmarium, which was situated at the very end of a long corridor beyond the chapterhouse and up against the Abbey walls.

Arriving at last at the solid door of the Infirmarium, Gabe turned the handle as gently as he could, knowing that it had needed oiling for many seasons now, and eased it open.

Through the crack that appeared, he could see Brother Archibold's desk, the wooden chair tucked in neatly, the wide timber surface empty but for an unlit candle stub. The Brother had gone to matins and Gabe's heart sank as he realized what that might mean.

Pushing the door open farther, Gabe stuck his head inside the room and his worst fears were confirmed. The six beds for the sick, lined up against the far wall, were all precisely made, the white linen on them pulled tight at the corners, glowing in the soft lamp light.

Gabe gulped as his eyes took in the fact that every bed was empty. Despite his faint hopes, Brother Benedict was not here. More tellingly, however, the Abbot was not here either.

Pulling the door gently closed, Gabe fled back down the long corridor, his mind racing. The Prior had lied. If the Abbot had been ill, as he'd said, then he would have been in one of those beds.

Gabe remembered Brother Archibold's deep frown at the chapterhouse meeting the day before, his assistance with getting Brother Malachy outside the room to help Gabe . . . It seemed that Gabe was not the only one with misgivings about the Abbot.

Now all Gabe could do was hope that Brother Malachy would make contact soon, so that they could decide what to do about the missing Abbot.

So consumed was he by his thoughts that Gabe almost failed to notice that the chanting within the chapterhouse had ended, and that his running feet were pounding on the stones. Immediately, Gabe slowed, creeping along, listening to the rise and fall of the Prior's voice as he led the end of matins.

Relief flooded through Gabe as he realized that he was nearing the hallway that would lead him back to the outer door and to Gwyn, and he quickened his pace once more as he rounded the corner – and ran straight into a solid chest.

"Oof!" he said, but managed to remember Gwyn's words and kept his face angled downward so his eyes could not be seen. All he could see now were a man's rough, callused feet and the dirty hem of a monk's habit. The man must be part of the stable or garden team,

Gabe decided, relieved – he didn't know any of them particularly well.

"Where are you going?" said an unfamiliar voice.

"The Necessarium," Gabe muttered.

"Who said you could leave prayers?" the voice demanded.

"Er, Brother Malachy," Gabe said, knowing that the kind older man would cover for him as much as possible, without actually lying.

The man grunted. "Very well," he said, standing aside, "but be quick."

Muttering his thanks, Gabe walked quickly away, wondering for a moment what the monk himself was doing outside matins, before dismissing it, preferring to concentrate on getting away from the Abbey before Damman or the Prior spotted him.

Finally, his ragged breathing loud in his ears, Gabe made one last turn and there it was – the door to freedom. And casually leaning against it was Gwyn, with a large bundle under her arm, waiting for him.

"What took you so long?" she hissed.

Gabe could do nothing but laugh quietly to himself as he followed her out the door, relief coursing through his body.

As he trudged up the hill behind her, he glanced back at the Abbey, its gray walls looking smaller and smaller the higher he walked. He remembered how safe he'd felt within those walls. Sadness bloomed within Gabe as he realized that he might never again find sanctuary there.

"Shh," said a loud voice, jolting Gabe from his slumber. Merry. He moaned and turned over in his bedroll. Surely it couldn't be morning already? He'd put his head on the pillow only moments ago.

"I will not *shh*," came Scarlett's indignant reply, and even Gabe had to hide a grin at the volume. The more time he spent with Scarlett, the more he suspected she'd had few people in her life who'd told her what to do.

"I'm awake," Gabe muttered, hearing noises that sounded as though Scarlett was being forcibly gagged. He sat up, rubbing sleep from his eyes, and discovered Merry's face just inches from his own. She was sitting on Scarlett.

"Good morrow," Merry said, quite as though they'd just met in passing on a country lane, completely ignoring the girl struggling beneath her. "We hope you had a restful night."

"No we don't," said Scarlett, sounding breathless, finally managing to roll out from under her cousin. "We hope they had a *successful* night."

"We did," said Gabe, before clarifying, "at least I think we did."

He glanced around the room.

"Gwyn's not here," said Merry, as though reading his mind. "Foraging, I'd say. We only knew you'd made it back because she left you here."

Gabe winced, feeling bone tired. "Did she sleep?" he asked.

"Gwyn's . . . restless," Merry said. "She's never slept much, and even less since Pa went away."

Scarlett's lips tightened into a moue of distaste. "She's always been strange, you mean," she said. "Father says she takes after your mother."

Merry elbowed her, a flash of anger in her amber eyes. "Yes, well he would say that," she said, "given he only inherited his title thanks to my mother." Scarlett frowned.

Wanting to break the uncomfortable pause that followed as the cousins glared at each other, Gabe blurted out the first question that came to mind. "Where *is* your mother?"

Merry rocked back on her heels, tucking her red hair behind her ear, the expression on her face making Gabe wish he hadn't opened his mouth.

"She's dead," Merry said, shortly. "Died birthing Gwyn."

"Oh," was all Gabe could manage, wondering if the burden of that was what had made Gwyn . . . the way she was. "Mine, too."

Merry's face softened. "Your ma died birthing you?" she asked.

"Yes," he said, before reconsidering. "Well, I think so. I was found on the Abbey steps, wrapped in a blanket with a note tucked inside."

"Ooh," said Scarlett, and Gabe noticed that she'd forgotten her antagonism towards her cousin and crept a little closer.

"What did the note say?" asked Merry.

"This here is Gabriel. Look after him," said Gabe, repeating what the Abbot had read to him once he was old enough to understand.

"Oh," said Scarlett, looking disappointed. "Is that all?"

Merry elbowed her again and fixed her with a hard stare. "That's enough," she said.

Gabe stared at his feet. He'd never really thought very much about his parents, but having said the words on the note out loud, he now realized how bald they were.

"Did they?" asked Scarlett, her courtly manners back in place. "Look after you, I mean?"

Gabe considered her question. He'd grown up in the Abbey, and knew every stone in the walls, every blade of grass, the face of every Brother, young and old. His life had simply gone on, day after day, and he'd been happy, surrounded by people who educated him, prayed for him, fed him and seemed to care for him. He'd never stopped to consider what he might be missing out on.

But Merry's expression when she talked about her ma and pa, and the determination that she and Gwyn had to save their father, suggested that maybe there was more to it. He looked at the cousins, sitting so closely that their shoulders were touching, and considered the easy physical familiarity between the girls. Nobody had ever thrown a casual arm around Gabe's shoulders.

"They did," he began slowly. "They did the best they could." Gabe realized the truth of his words as he spoke them. Until two years before when Prior Dismas had arrived, replacing Prior James who'd left to be Abbot at another Abbey, Gabe had been very happy.

His education had begun as soon as he could walk and talk and he'd loved the more formal schooling he'd done from the ages of six to ten. The next two years had been spent trying out different sections of Abbey life, looking for the perfect fit for the time when he would take his vows and become a Brother himself. He had settled into the Scriptorium, with regular visits to Brother Benedict in the Librarium, even though part of his heart remained in the Herbarium.

Strange to think that only two days before, that decision had been the biggest problem he'd ever had . . .

But talking about his parents had stirred up emotions for which Gabe had no name. "What about you?" he asked Scarlett, trying to divert attention away from himself. "Why are you here?"

Scarlett bit her bottom lip. "I'm – I was – to be married," she said. "To a friend of my father's."

"How old are you?" he asked, aghast.

"Fifteen," she admitted. "Old enough to be married, but . . ."

Merry put her arm around her cousin. "Scarlett's a romantic," she said, "she believes in courtly love and poetry. Her father is more interested in an alliance with a powerful family."

"He sold me!" Scarlett said, her face red with indignation, though Gabe saw the stormy sadness in her eyes. "Like a cow in the barn. To the highest bidder."

"There, there," said Merry, patting her arm, "it's all over now. You're safe here with us."

"He must never find me," said Scarlett, her fists clenched in her lap. "I would rather die than go back."

"Nobody's dying," came Gwyn's voice from the door. "Not today." She strode into the room and dumped a bag at Scarlett's feet. "I found some of those field mushrooms you like so much. See if Midge can make them into a soup – a nice, *thick* soup, mind."

"Mmm," said Scarlett, pulling a large, creamy mushroom from the bag and sniffing it as though she would inhale it without chewing. "I'll take them to her now. She's out back."

"I know," said Gwyn, also sniffing the air. "I can smell the bread."

It took her words for Gabe to realize how hungry he was and that it was the tantalizing scent of baked bread that was making him so. He tried to remember the last time he'd eaten – it felt like days ago.

With Scarlett gone, Gwyn's watchful expression reappeared. "He tell you anything?" she asked Merry.

"We were getting to it," said Merry, without looking at Gabe, who was beginning to feel as though he'd disappeared into thin air. "We got distracted. You delivered the note?"

Gwyn rolled her eyes as though this was the silliest question ever.

"And you," Merry continued, now turning her attention to Gabe, "you left the cover?"

Gabe nodded, momentarily reliving the tide of fear that had risen within him as he'd traveled through the halls he'd once thought so safe.

"Well, then," Merry said, dusting her hands together with a satisfied expression. "Now we wait."

"Wait?" said Gwyn. "For what? You said his part of the deal was to help us rescue Pa. We should get on with that."

"We'll wait to hear from this Malachy," said Merry. "We'll wait for news. Then we'll decide on a plan."

"And in the meantime?" asked Gwyn, arms folded across her chest. "What will we do while we wait?"

"Ah, now, Gwyn, don't fret," said Merry, putting an arm around her sister with a smile. "A little birdie told me this morning that Goodwife Alice has just had her babe and that the family requires some help."

To Gabe's surprise, Gwyn's face brightened and he wondered if he'd judged her too harshly. Anyone who looked so pleased to be able to help others couldn't be all bad.

"So we forage for food?" he asked, pleased to have something useful to do to block out his own problems.

Merry laughed. "Something like that," she said. "I've got a plan – and you're going to be just right for it."

Looking at the gleeful expression on Gwyn's face, Gabe suddenly had a very bad feeling.

CHAPTER SIX

"This is completely dishonest," said Gabe, writhing about in the dirt. "I can't do this – and neither should you!"

"So you said," said Scarlett, kneeling on his chest and tying the last knot. "Don't fret. Merry's given you the perfect role. None of this can be your fault."

She stood and left him lying in the middle of the dusty road, miserably aware that he must look like a chicken trussed up for baking. Like the bait that he was.

Merry's plan, it had turned out, was simple. Gabe would be positioned on the main road between Featherstone, the nearest village, and Rothwell, feigning injury. When an innocent passerby stopped to assist him, the other four – as even Midge was in on this despicable act – would knock out the stranger and rob him. They'd then all run away.

Gabe had shaken his head. "No," he said. "I cannot do it. I will not do it. It's wrong."

"It's not for us, silly!" Merry had said. "It's for Goodwife Alice and her bairns. She lost her husband not three months ago and this is her fifth babe. She's got naught."

Horrified at the unknown woman's plight, Gabe had hesitated.

"See," said Merry. "You can see how wrong that is. She can't work her plot so she won't be able to pay her tithe. If she can't pay her tithe, Lord Lah-di-da will toss her out on her ear, like he's done to so many others! Then where will they all go?"

Now all four girls were staring at him, woebegone expressions on their faces, even Gwyn's, and he realized they really did care about this woman and her fate.

"But to rob an innocent person?" Gabe said. "That's not the way to go about helping her."

"What would you suggest then?" said Gwyn, striding over to poke him in the chest. "Got the answers, do you? Know how to get her off the streets and keep the bairns out of the *foundling home?*" The emphasis she placed on these last words suggested that, for Gwyn, there was no worse place to be.

"Have you been to a foundling home?" he asked. Gabe had heard of foundling homes, thanks to Damman, who'd taken great pleasure in telling him that had Gabe been dumped on the Abbey steps today he'd have been shipped off to the closest foundling home.

Gabe had questioned Brother Malachy about this information and discovered that Damman was right: the Abbeys had stopped taking in orphaned children, simply because these days there were so many.

Once, Rothwell and its surrounding countryside had been a prosperous, peaceful place to live. But then Lord Sherborne had inherited the castle in the walled town from his father and things had begun to change as taxes had grown higher and higher, farming families had begun to starve and gangs of brigands had begun roving the quiet country lanes.

Then came the whispers, even behind the high walls of the Abbey, of men and women disappearing – anyone who voiced a protest, an opinion, a thought against Lord Sherborne . . .

"We have been to a foundling home," said Merry now, coming to stand behind her sister, "and trust me, we're never going back. And neither are Goodwife Alice's bairns. Not while we can help it."

As the plan had unfolded, it became clear to Gabe that none of the girls had any intention of keeping any of the profits of the robbery for themselves. It was all to go to Goodwife Alice.

"Do you, er, do this often?" he'd asked, as Merry drew a map of everyone's position in the dirt outside the tree.

"Often enough," was all she said, before continuing with her plan.

But, at the last moment, standing by the roadside, Gabe had balked, unable to go through with his part when it would result in the injury of another.

"It's not right," he said.

"We only choose rich travelers," Scarlett reasoned. "We wait for hours sometimes, letting everyone else pass by without even knowing we're here. But the rich can afford it."

"But you hurt them!" Gabe said.

"Just a little," Merry soothed, stepping closer to put an arm around him, her cloak flapping around her ankles. The long bow held in her other hand made the position awkward.

Gabe opened his mouth to respond, but before he could get a sound out, Merry had kicked the legs out from under him and Gabe hit the ground with a thud.

"Wrap him," she said, and Gwyn was on him, looping a rope around and around him, tying him up tight.

"Sorry, Gabe," Merry continued, her voice light but that steel back in her eyes. "Goodwife Alice is counting on us and we don't like to let people down."

And so here he was, gagged and bound, awaiting an unsuspecting traveler.

"Masks on – get ready," he heard Gwyn hiss from behind a nearby honeysuckle shrub at almost exactly the same time that he became aware of a dull thudding vibrating through the dirt under his head. Her instincts were uncanny, he realized, just as Merry's planning was impeccable.

She'd chosen a dip in the road just around the bend from a stone bridge. The incline down to the bridge was long and relatively steep, meaning that any traveler, be they in a cart, on horseback or on foot, would have to slow down as they reached the bridge, so as to traverse its narrow path. They would still be moving relatively slowly as they rounded the bend and would be almost on top of him before they realized it.

Even as Gabe was thinking this, he heard the rumbling of wheels and then a loud "Whoa!" and a flurry of hooves and wheels in the dirt as the horse and cart – for his limited view meant he had to assume that's what it was – squealed to a halt. There was a moment's silence and then a man's rough voice shouted: "What the devil!"

Gabe writhed in the dirt, trying to remove his gag so he could warn the man.

"Slocum, what is it?" came a squeaky female voice, and Gabe rapidly recalculated, realizing that Merry's trap had netted a horse and *carriage*.

"Monk on the road, m'lady," said an unexpectedly rough voice, and Gabe frowned beneath his gag. His work in the guest lodgings at the Abbey had brought him into contact with the drivers of fine carriages before and most of them sounded like a poor imitation of the nobles that they ferried about in their fine carriages.

This man sounded more like a peasant who had hitched a ride on the back of a merchant's cart or arrived footsore after walking many miles. The fact that he didn't immediately recognize that Gabe was not a full monk was another cause for concern.

Something was not right here – he needed to warn the girls.

"Hmmph, hmmph." Feeing his face grow red, Gabe realized that trying to scream behind a gag was getting him nowhere.

"Move him out of the way," squeaked the woman in the carriage and Gabe heard the driver jump down into the dirt as the horse stamped and whinnied.

Heavy footsteps moved towards him and Gabe began to throw himself about as violently as he could, trying to caterpillar his way across the road, but only succeeding in getting dirt up his nose and in his ears.

One step – two steps – the man was almost upon him and that meant, Gabe knew, that the girls would soon show themselves. He couldn't fully explain why, but somehow he knew that Merry's trap was being turned against her and the others – this was a trap for them!

As the man stood over him, Gabe reacted without thinking, gathering up both his legs and thrusting them at the man's groin. The driver fell backward onto the road with a howl of pain, which was cut short when his head hit the dirt with a thud, and he lay still. Gabe blinked, hoping that he hadn't inflicted pain on a man who turned out to be innocent. But no, now Gabe heard the sound of doors opening – not one, not two, but four – and the shouts of many men.

He'd been right!

Gabe's moment of jubilation was squashed in an instant by a rush of fear – what had he done? He might have saved the girls, but now he was lying completely helpless in the face of whatever came next. For surely the girls would have run at first sight of these men?

Gabe's anxious thoughts were interrupted by a whizzing, pinging sound and he rolled onto his side to see arrows raining down into the space between him and the feet of the men approaching. The feet stopped.

"Drop your swords!" said Merry, but there was no cheerful lilt in her voice now. "Drop them or I'll shoot you all where you stand."

There was a moment's hesitation and Gabe could hear shuffling feet as the men looked around them, trying to work out where Merry's voice was coming from. Then another flurry of arrows rained down, landing in a perfect line close to the men's toes.

"You don't want to see where the next ones go," said Merry.

This time there was no hesitation and the men's swords dropped one by one, clanging into the dirt.

"Good," came Merry's voice. "Face forward, eyes front. First man who looks anywhere but down the road will die."

To illustrate her point, another line of arrows hit the dirt, this time barely missing the tops of the men's boots.

"Ben, Will, tie them," she said, and Gabe wondered who she was talking to.

As Gabe watched, still able to see only feet, he saw Gwyn's boots, followed by Scarlett's, creep up behind the men, who cursed in turn as the girls tied their hands behind their backs. As soon as they were done, the boots crept away.

Gabe tucked away the fact that Merry had used boys' names instead of the girls' own names – something Scarlett had not yet learned to do.

"Who sent you?" Merry demanded of the men, who stood silent. She chuckled, low in her throat, and dispatched just one arrow, which hit the nearest man squarely in the ankle, making him wail with pain. "Who sent you?" Merry demanded again.

"Ronan of Feldham," said the next man in the line, hastily, whilst the others cursed him.

"Why are you here?" Merry asked.

"To find you," said another voice, sullenly. "Ronan is unhappy with your crime spree."

Merry chuckled again. "Oh ho!" she said. "It's a spree now, is it?"

"Four innocent travelers robbed in as many weeks," said the same voice. "I'd call that a spree."

"Hmm," said Merry, noncommittally. "What if I told you this was the first time we'd done this?"

"Ha!" said the same voice, and Gabe realized this was the leader of the group. "We know."

"How?" Merry demanded, but the man simply laughed.

"How?" she asked again, but now her question was accompanied by another arrow, this time into the ankle of the next man in line.

"Your arrows!" he gasped, despite the leader's best efforts to drown out his answer with a shout. "Your arrows are distinctive!"

Merry said nothing, but Gabe could almost feel her taking that on board. He wondered what she would do next – surely she didn't mean to kill these men? Wounding them was one thing but . . .

As though in answer to his thoughts, Merry spoke again. "Turn around," she said.

The men did as they were told.

"Start walking," she said.

"Where to?" the man on the far end of the line said.

"Back to Rothwell," said Merry. "Tell Ronan of Feldham that I send my regards."

"But who *are* you?" asked the leader, craftily.

Merry laughed, a delighted giggle that danced across the road above Gabe's head. "Oh, but that would be telling," she said. "Tell Ronan of Feldham I'll be pleased to make formal introductions when the time is right. Now, walk."

"It's a very long way," whined one of the injured men.

"It is," Merry agreed, pleasantly. "Best you get going then."

"But what about our friend?" asked the leader, indicating the man still lying in the road.

"Never fear," said Merry, still hidden somewhere in the bushes. "The Monk will look after him."

Gabe frowned, unsure what he was supposed to do with the still man lying beside him, but his aggravation was quickly replaced when he noticed that the other four men were walking away, trudging towards Rothwell, two of them dragging clearly painful ankles behind them.

Gabe waited, wondering if the girls would come and untie him now that the men had left, but all was silent, bar the birds twittering in the nearby trees and an occasional jingle from the horse's bridle as it stood patiently awaiting instruction.

Time passed and Gabe began to sweat as the sun rose in the sky. Had the girls abandoned him? He *had* let them down by refusing to pretend to be injured – but surely he'd redeemed himself?

Just as he was beginning to give up hope, wondering if they'd simply left him here to be returned to Oldham Abbey to face Prior Dismas and his fate, Gabe heard Gwyn's low voice.

"Now," was all she said. With that, the girls were around him, Merry and Scarlett kneeling to untie him, Gwyn standing guard over the other man, and Midge talking to the horse in a calm, quiet voice

"Sorry about that," said Merry. "We had to be sure they'd gotten far enough away."

"They're still arguing about whether it's worse to die from an arrow to the heart or to face Ronan and tell him that not only did they not catch you, but they lost a horse and carriage as well . . ." said Gwyn, who'd clearly followed the men. "So I'd suggest we get on with it."

"Are you able to walk?" Merry asked, pulling Gabe to his feet. Looking into her concerned face, Gabe wondered if he'd imagined that low menacing voice, those arrows . . . How could one person have two such different sides? But all he said was, "I'm all right."

"Right, Midgey, you ride the horse and meet us back at the oak," said Merry. Midge nodded and Gabe noticed that she'd already untethered the beast from the carriage.

"I'll need a boost," she said, and Scarlett kneeled beside her, hands clasped together. As Gabe watched, Midge put one foot in the loop Scarlett had created and, as Scarlett stood, Midge gracefully vaulted up and landed lightly on the horse's back. Grasping the huge animal's mane, she leaned forward and seemed to whisper in its ear. The horse whinnied and walked out between the carriage shafts.

Midge patted it on the neck, before touching her heel to its side. The horse obediently turned and walked down towards the trees lining the road. As it disappeared into the woods at a delicate trot, Midge turned and waved, the smile on her face as wide as an April moon.

"We're taking the horse?" Gabe asked.

"It's the only thing of value here," Merry explained. "And it will fetch a pretty penny."

"But how will you sell it?" Gabe asked in amazement.

"We know someone," was all Merry said, and Gabe shook his head. He thought about what the Abbot would have to say about all this – stealing was wrong. But then he thought about Goodwife Alice and her children and the fate that would befall them without any help – surely that was wrong, too?

"Don't fret, Gabe," Merry said. "You didn't do anything wrong here – you were tied up."

"If anything," Scarlett said, "you were a hero and you saved us. How did you know something was wrong?"

"The driver," Gabe said. "He had the wrong voice."

Merry smiled. "And here Gwyn was thinking you were useless."

Gabe frowned. Useless? He could do lots of things – read, write, draw, and . . .

He stopped. All of the things he could do were of great use in the Abbey, in his world. But out here?

Out here, he realized with a sigh, useful skills were things like tracking and foraging, hunting and shooting, planning and bargaining.

Which was why he needed to stick with these girls, whether the Abbot would agree with their outlook or not.

"Gwyn's not always right, surely," was all he said in response to Merry.

"No," said Merry. "But she's not usually wrong either. You're a bit of an unknown quantity, Sandals, to all of us."

"As you are to me," Gabe said, wondering if all girls were like these four. He'd seen girls from a distance, of course, but he'd never actually spoken to any.

Merry laughed. "Indeed! All right, enough chatter, let's get home."

"What about him?" Gabe asked, indicating the man still lying in the road.

"He'll be fine," said Gwyn, "he's breathing strongly. I'd say he'll be awake by the time those others turn back to get him. Help me get him into the carriage, out of the sun."

Gabe took the man's feet as Scarlett and Gwyn took a shoulder each, and they manhandled his dead weight onto the floor of the plush carriage.

"Dust at the top of the hill," Merry reported. "We've got company."

And with that, she was gone, disappearing into the trees like a wisp of smoke, Scarlett at her heels, Gwyn nowhere to be seen.

Pulling up the hem of his robe, Gabe looked right and left down the road before following them.

Later that night, Gabe sat quietly, his back against the mighty oak tree, staring out into the impenetrable darkness of the trees. The contrast between the bright moonlight that illuminated the clearing around him, and the gloom of those trees was marked.

Somewhere above him, Albert shifted on his perch. Midge kept him tethered to a wide branch with thin leather straps called jesses. Watching from below as she'd knotted the end around Albert's leg earlier, Gabe had noted that she used the same complicated sequence that Brother Gilbert used.

"Where did you learn to do that?" he called up to her.

"My papa always had birds," she said, giving Albert's sleek feathers one last stroke before climbing back down. "He loved animals, like I do."

When Gabe had asked her how long she'd owned Albert, Midge had smiled. "I don't own him," she said. "I found him injured in the woods and he chooses to stay with me. One day he'll go."

Now, the girls were lying on their backs out in the center of the clearing, staring up at the stars, talking in low voices. The horse had gone, taken away by a tall bearded man in a long gray cloak not long after Gabe had returned to the oak. Midge had almost wept to see it go, but the man had promised her that he would see to it the horse went to a good home.

Gabe had not seen how much money was in the small bag that the man had given Merry, but the chink as he'd dropped it into her hand suggested that the horse had, in fact, fetched a "pretty penny" as Merry had predicted.

Gwyn had taken the bag from Merry almost at once, secured it to her belt under a traveling cloak, and disappeared into the trees, returning without the bag just before sundown.

"All's well?" Merry asked Gwyn, as Midge had served up a tasty vegetable stew.

"Aye," Gwyn had responded, and Gabe had been struck by the sweetness of her smile. It was as though the sun had come out from behind storm clouds.

"You told her?" Merry continued.

"Aye," Gwyn said again. "I told her a man gave it to me to give to her."

Merry smiled. "Good. And she knows –"

"She'll hide it safe," Gwyn interrupted. "She'll only spend a little at a time. She knows. She cried."

"They always do," Merry said, her own expression serene.

"Oh, let me do the next one!" Scarlett had said. "I want to see it for my own eyes."

"Maybe," Merry answered, not looking at her cousin, and Gabe knew, even if Scarlett did not, that it would never be Scarlett's turn. Even Gabe could see that it would be foolhardy to send such a memorable face.

"Are you okay?" Midge asked, breaking into his thoughts.

"I'm fine," he sighed, moving over a little to make room for the small girl to sit beside him.

"I know how you feel," she said, her dark eyes searching his. "I remember my first time, too. You're torn between the good and the bad of this, aren't you?"

He looked down into her earnest little face. She looked so young – too young to be holding people up on the Rothwell Road.

"People got hurt today," was all he said.

"They did," she said. "But those men – men like them – did much worse to my mama and papa."

"It was soldiers who killed your parents?" Gabe whispered.

"It was." Midge nodded. "I don't know whose soldiers they were because I can't remember much from that day. Merry says I've blanked it out of my mind, and she must be right. But I know they were soldiers because Papa called out something like 'we'll tell the Lord's knights' and they laughed and said, 'We *are* his knights.'"

Gabe was silent. "Even so," he said, "piling on wrongs doesn't help anyone."

"Merry wouldn't do the wrong thing," Midge said, fiercely. "She would never kill innocent people for no reason – not like those soldiers did to my parents. She would never kill anyone at all, except to save one of us."

Gabe gasped. "She's killed someone?"

"No!" Midge shouted, and Gabe saw the other three lift their heads in his direction. "She never has and she never would – unless it was to save her pa or one of us."

Gabe looked down at Midge with compassion, understanding the girl's loyalty to her friend. "But what if she makes a mistake? Any one of those arrows today could have gone wrong and killed someone by mistake."

Midge laughed, a wonderful, clear sound that rang around the clearing. "Merry's arrows only ever go where Merry wants them to go."

Gabe frowned, cocking his head. "How can you say that?"

Midge looked at him, a smug expression on her face. "I just can," she said. "And what's more, at first light tomorrow, I'll get her to prove it to you."

It was still dark when Gabe sat up, wondering what had woken him. Around him, the girls also stirred.

And then the bells began again, pealing their triumph far and wide.

"What is it?" Scarlett asked, lighting a candle and rubbing her eyes.

"Ringing the changes," Gabe said, listening to the joyous sounds, picturing Brothers Simeon, Gilbert, Altus and Percival clinging to the bell ropes in the ringing chamber, fiercely concentrating on the pattern in which the bells were rung. Normally, Gabe would be with them, as the smallest and youngest member of the bell-ringing team. But not today. He wondered who had taken his place on the rope for the treble bell.

"What does it mean?" Midge asked. "What's happened?"

"I think," Gabe responded slowly, looking around at their anxious faces, "it means they've found the golden book – or think they have, because they have the cover."

"Would they really ring the bells for that?" Scarlett asked. "I thought it was kept for special news."

Gabe thought back to Brother Benedict's disappearance, Prior Dismas's search for the book, and Dammon's words to Gabe in the forest. "It *is* special," he said. "I wish . . ." He stopped, feeling his status as a fugitive from the Abbey keenly.

"Wish what?" prompted Merry.

"That I knew what was happening," Gabe said, looking around at their perplexed faces in the flickering candlelight. "I don't understand any of this."

Merry stood. "Well, I think it's time for Gwyn to pay a visit to a certain horse," she said. "See if there's any information from that Brother of yours."

"Malachy," Gabe supplied automatically.

"Malachy," Merry repeated, before turning to her sister. "Sun won't be up for a few hours yet. Take Midge, in case the horse gives you trouble."

Gwyn nodded, and Midge stood without saying a word and followed her out of the room.

"What about me?" Gabe asked, watching them go. "I should go."

"If they're ringing bells, the entire Abbey will be crawling with people," said Merry. "Until we know more, you're safest here – and so is that book that you refuse to take out of your pocket."

It was true. Merry had suggested hiding the book in the hollow oak, assuring Gabe that no one would find it, but Gabe would have none of it. "Brother Benedict gave it to me for safekeeping," he'd told her several times now. "He said not to let it out of my sight. It's staying with me."

He'd had reason to wonder about that decision whilst lying in the middle of the Rothwell Road yesterday, but now, feeling the heavy weight of the book tucked against his leg, he was glad.

"Nothing to do but wait then," said Merry. "Roll over and get some sleep. Gwyn and Midge will be a while yet."

Sleep? thought Gabe, as Merry blew out the candle and he heard her and Scarlett slide down into their sleeping rolls. Outside, the bells maintained their distant joyous caroling, but inside, the girls' rustling was soon replaced by deep, steady breaths, suggesting they'd both dropped off.

Gabe lay awake, staring up into the darkness, one hand on the book beside him, his mind whirling. There was no way he'd be getting any more sleep tonight.

"Gabe, Gabe." Midge's gentle voice was accompanied by a light shake to Gabe's shoulder.

"Wha–?" Gabe sat bolt upright, blinking at the bright sunlight streaming through the high, tiny windows cut into the oak tree's trunk.

"Typical Sandals," came Gwyn's dispassionate voice. "Sleeping while other people get the work done. Here."

She dropped something into Gabe's lap, sauntering from the room before he could manage a response to her unfair statement.

"Don't mind her," said Midge. "It took longer than we'd hoped and she hates that."

"Are you okay?" he asked, worried. "Did someone see you?"

"Oh no." Midge laughed. "Gwyn would never allow that. It's just that the horses must have been frightened by the bells and so one of the – not a Brother, more like you . . ."

"A novice?" Gabe said.

"Yes, a novice – he was sleeping in the loose box with Borlan, which made it much harder to get the note."

Gabe smiled. "That would have been Nicholas," he said. "He loves that horse."

Midge giggled. "We could see that," she said. "He was tucked up beside it like they were family. I thought it was lovely but Gwyn . . ." She didn't need to finish.

"So what did you do?" he asked.

"We waited a while – we'd climbed up the outside of the stable and into the hayloft – but then Gwyn was worried that the rooster would crow and the stables would fill with people, so we decided that I would go down and have a look around."

Gabe felt his eyebrows fly up his forehead. "How did you do that without waking Nicholas?"

Midge smiled modestly, though her eyes twinkled mischievously. "I'm only little, so Gwyn lowered me down on a rope that was up in the hayloft. Your Brother Malachy is clever – he'd tucked the note behind Borlan's nameplate on the door of the box."

"How did you even think to look there?"

"It made sense – you wouldn't put it in the straw or the feed box in case Borlan ate it by mistake and you couldn't hide it on the actual horse. You said that you'd told Brother Malachy to leave the answer with Borlan so . . . with his name seemed the best bet."

Gabe shook his head in amazement, wondering if he would have worked all that out in such a short space of time.

"Anyway," Midge continued, "I'll leave you to read it. We'll wait outside."

She backed away with such reverence that Gabe was confused. Before meeting these girls, he'd never really thought much about reading and writing. It was simply something that every boy at the Abbey had to learn and they started at a young age. Brother Simeon, who taught the very young boys, had always told them it was a privilege but, frankly, hours and hours of repeating words and sounds had felt more like a prison, something that had to be gotten through before they'd finally be released into the courtyard to play for a while.

But he was beginning to see that Brother Simeon was right. Something that he'd treated as a chore was seen as truly magical by the girls, who would never have had an opportunity to take the lessons that he had. Had they had any schooling at all? Gabe would ask them later, but he suspected they had not.

In the meantime, however, there was Brother Malachy's letter to read, and Gabe opened it eagerly. There was no name on the letter and it was unsigned, but he recognized the firm strokes of the lettering immediately.

I have no idea how you got your message to me, nor if this response will ever be collected. I can only hope that it is not discovered by others before it is found by you.

Gabe smiled, imagining Brother Malachy's surprise at discovering the original note.

I have racked my brains for the man you asked about and can think of no one. There has been no sign of the other and I fear that a great evil has been visited upon us.

If Brother Malachy did not know of Aidan, then Gabe could think of no one else who would. What had Brother Benedict been thinking? And what had happened to him as a result of his actions? And the Abbot?

> *The bells sounded last night to give news of a great discovery, but I think you will know what has been found. Know this, the glittering clothes were but the face and it is the heart that is truly sought. Keep it safe.*
>
> *In the absence of our leader, do not come here again lest you also disappear.*

Gabe swallowed hard, turning the letter over, but there was no more.

So Prior Dismas was celebrating the discovery of the golden book that Gabe had planted in the Librarium, all the while knowing that it was not the book he sought. Who was he trying to deceive and why? And what was it about the book in Gabe's pocket that was so important?

Gabe reread the last line of the letter, his heart sinking. Brother Malachy's warning was stark against the pale vellum. *Do not come here again.* The Abbot was still missing and it was not safe for Gabe to return to the Abbey, to his old life and his home. Which meant . . . that he had nowhere to go.

There had been boys who'd run away from the Abbey in the past. Novices who'd changed their minds, oblates whose families had paid a high price for the Abbot to take their sons without ever asking those sons what they'd wanted. As far as Gabe could remember, all of those boys had returned, weeping, to the Abbey, after finding out that the big adventures they'd sought outside the walls were not as wonderful as they'd imagined – or discovering that the family the boys had so desperately missed did not want them back.

But Gabe, who had never wanted to leave, would never be able to return.

He folded the vellum carefully, following the creases already in place, his mind whirling as hot tears pricked the backs of his eyes. What had Brother Benedict been thinking, giving the book to him? Surely there would have been someone else, someone more suitable?

"Gabe?" whispered Merry, and he turned to see her, silhouetted against the bright sunlight streaming through the open door, her backlit hair creating a fiery halo around her head. "Are you all right?"

Gabe wiped his eyes with the back of his hand. "I am," he said. "I think. I'm . . ." His words trailed away.

"What did he say?" she asked, coming in to sit beside him.

Unable to look at her, Gabe stared at the wall, repeating the letter almost word for word. She was silent.

"I'm not sure what to do," he admitted.

Merry jumped to her feet and began to pace up and down the room. She and her sister were unalike in so many ways, he thought, watching her. Gwyn was almost unnaturally still most of the time, keeping her thoughts to herself behind that closed face. Merry, on the other hand, was always on the move and often walked as she talked. "Way I see it, you've got two choices," she was saying. "You can either do as he says and stay away, sell the book and build a new life for yourself somewhere."

Gabe opened his mouth to speak, horrified at the notion of selling the book, even more horrified at the idea of being alone and starting again.

"Or," Merry continued, holding up one hand to quiet him, "you find this Aidan, discover the secret of the book, expose the Prior for the cheat and liar that he is, return the book to the Abbey and go back to the way things were."

"Isn't there a third option?" Gabe whispered, his mouth suddenly dry. "I mean, I'm not sure that either of those would work."

Merry laughed. "Of course," she said. "Third option, you take your book, run back to the Abbey, let Ronan of Feldham take you to the castle dungeon as a thief, and you're never heard from again."

"That would be my preferred option," came Gwyn's voice from the door. "Then we could all go back to the task of rescuing Pa rather than running around on a fool's mission."

"Hush, Gwyn," said Merry. "It's not his fault that he's a babe in the woods, and you know he won't survive a minute out here without us."

Listening to the two of them bickering about him like he wasn't in the room, Gabe was hit by a wave of anger. It wasn't his fault that he was here. He hadn't asked for any of it – not even their help. In the past three days he'd been jumped on, chased, tied up, threatened, and dragged into a mystery that was very likely going to get him killed, and now these girls were talking about him like he was a baby.

He slowly got to his feet. "I would, you know," Gabe said, trying to sound more certain than he felt as they turned to look at him. "Survive, I mean. Oh, maybe I can't sneak around in the dark like Gwyn or shoot arrows like you, Merry, but I can read and I can write and I can count. I know how to sing, how to grow food and how to clean out stables."

As he spoke, Gabe could feel his confidence growing. Life at the Abbey may not have prepared him entirely for life outside its walls, but there was no doubt that he had skills – and useful skills at that, having done his time in every section of the Abbey.

"Well, well," said Merry, with a half smile. "Sandals has a backbone, Gwyn."

"I was wondering if we'd see one," Gwyn agreed, nodding, the expression on her sharp little features almost proud.

"And what do you propose to do with all these things you can do?" Merry asked, walking towards him.

"I, er, don't know," said Gabe, deflating a little. "Find work?"

"You're just going to wander into Featherstone and offer yourself up, are you?" asked Gwyn, a little smile playing around her lips.

Gabe frowned. "Why is that funny?" he asked, looking to Merry for an answer.

Merry laughed. "The fact that you don't even know it's funny is what's funny," she said. "Word will have gone out, Gabe. Your Prior, Sheriff Ronan . . . they'll have sent riders to every village in walking or riding distance, offering a reward for you. They want that book. And that means that if you appear anywhere, they'll soon know about it."

"But how will they know it's me?" Gabe asked. "If I change my robes, put on something like you've got on, I'll look different."

Merry sighed. "You will definitely be doing that," she said. "But it won't be enough. There'll be a picture, Gabe, posted in the square of every town and village within riding distance. That's what they do. That's what happened to Pa."

"A picture?" Gabe queried. "What kind of picture?"

"A portrait," said Gwyn, with a certain amount of glee. "One of your monks will have painted a picture of you and there'll be a copy of it everywhere. With a reward on it."

"Don't fret," said Merry, seeing the look on his face. "Scarlett's got one – her father hasn't given up looking for her. Pa had one – before they found him, of course."

"But not us," said Gwyn, sounding triumphant and moving over to slide an arm around her sister's waist. "Nobody's looking for us."

"Well, they are," said Merry, "they just don't know it's us."

Gabe wondered what all this meant. He'd been branded a thief and now every person in every town and village would know it – and be out to claim the reward. There was no way for him to find work or even leave this forest without being caught.

"Are you okay?" he heard Merry ask, as a peculiar feeling of lightheadedness came over him and he slumped back to the ground, sitting cross-legged on his sleeping roll.

"I'm . . . not sure," Gabe admitted.

"You can stay here with us," Merry rushed to reassure him, "for as long as you need to. We'll keep you safe."

Gabe nodded weakly, unable to look at Gwyn's face. "Just a few more days," he said, "until I work out what to do next."

He heard Gwyn snort as she sauntered from the room and couldn't help but think she was right to be disbelieving. The truth was, Gabe had a secret book, a price on his head and no idea where to even start solving his problems.

CHAPTER SEVEN

Gabe turned the page listlessly, knowing even as he did so that he would simply be looking at yet more mumbo jumbo. Sure enough, another beautiful illustration, this time of a plant that looked a bit like a snowdrop, but with a drop of gold at its center.

"Anything?" asked Scarlett, coming over to lie on the grass beside him. It had been two days since Gabe had read Brother Malachy's letter and the girls were still tiptoeing around him like he had an illness. In a way, Gabe thought, it was as though he did, so sad and tired did he feel.

"Nothing," he said now, moving over slightly to allow Scarlett to see the book. "See – it's just these strange words and pictures, over and over."

Scarlett sighed, tossing her long fair braid over her shoulder. "I'd hoped there might be some mention of this Aidan you're looking for," she said, her face perplexed. "I was so sure."

It had been Scarlett who'd suggested that Gabe read through the book, looking for clues. The girls had allowed him to mope around for an hour or so before Merry had dragged him out into the clearing for the promised display of her archery skills.

Thoughts of his problems had fled as she'd made him stand, quivering, in front of the hollow oak with a pear balanced on his head.

Making a great show of drawing the arrow up to her chin and taking long, slow aim, Merry had suddenly let the arrow fly and, before he could even gasp, Gabe felt the arrow ruffle his hair and the twang as it hit the tree behind him, the pear neatly split in two.

Gabe was still blinking in disbelief when she'd strolled over and, grabbing one half of the pear, taken a big bite.

"Where did you learn to do that?" he'd whispered.

"Pa taught me," Merry said and her face creased with sadness. "He taught Gwyn as well, but she's better at other things."

"Will you teach me?" Gabe asked, thinking that if he was going to be on his own he might need to learn a few new things.

Merry laughed. "I can show you how," she said, "but it takes a long time to get good at it."

"Then let's start right now," he said eagerly, all thoughts of secrets and books fleeing his mind.

Later, he lay in the shade of the oak wondering if he'd ever be able to move his arms again, so tired and sore were they from holding the unfamiliar weight of the longbow. Gabe decided that, like most things, shooting an arrow looked incredibly easy when done by someone who did it well. In his hands, the bow had been an unwieldy mess of timber and string, whereas Merry made it look like an extension of her very person.

He'd just made the decision to get up early the following morning to practice on his own, without Gwyn's amused eyes on him, when Scarlett had approached him with her suggestion – and he'd spent the remainder of that day and most of this one combing every page of the manuscript.

"It's okay," Gabe said now. "I thought there might be clues in here as well. But . . ." He paused, flicking the pages. "I think it's a cipher," he said, slowly.

"What's a cipher?" said Scarlett, leaning in to look at the page he had open. "I've never heard of that."

"I've heard about them but . . . I thought they were a myth," Gabe said. "It's a book written in code."

"Why would anyone write something like that?" she asked. "Isn't the whole point of a book to be read?"

Gabe gulped. "A cipher holds secrets so great and powerful that they need to be kept safe," he said.

Scarlett sat back and stared at him. "There must be a key to the code, though?" she said. "What would be the point otherwise?"

"There doesn't seem to be anything in the book," said Gabe, his voice rising in frustration. "I'm worried that Prior Dismas has it — and now he just needs the cipher to complete the puzzle."

"Good enough reason to keep it hidden, then," said Scarlett, stretching her long legs out and rolling over onto her back, staring up at the sky. "I think you should know that we're all planning to go to Rothwell tomorrow," she said, after a pause. "Merry wants you to go, but Gwyn says no."

Gabe sat up. "Merry wants me to go?" he said, surprised.

"She's got this idea that you can help us to get to their pa," said Scarlett.

Gabe remembered the "deal" that Merry had made with him on his very first day in the forest.

"Gwyn thinks it's too dangerous — for you and for us. People are looking for you and if you're spotted, we'll be spotted."

"And Merry?" Gabe asked. Having spent more time with the red-haired girl, he'd come to admire not only her skill with a bow, but the patience and good humor with which she was helping him to get better with the weapon, making him take breaks from the book to practice.

She'd taught Gabe to focus down the shaft of his arrow, not just on the target, but on a tiny detail of the target. "Pa told me that if you're aiming to shoot a black rabbit, you don't aim for the rabbit, you aim for the one white hair on that rabbit," Merry told him.

When Gabe found his arrows were always flying to the right of where he was aiming, she laughed. "Your problem is that you're letting go of the string," she told him, "and that makes your arrow lurch."

"How else will it work?" he'd asked. "I have to let go or the arrow doesn't go anywhere."

"No," Merry said, taking the bow from him and drawing an arrow up to her chin, "you don't let go. Watch my hand. You just relax your fingers the tiniest bit and . . ."

Gabe blinked as the arrow left the bow and flew straight and true to the center of the target she'd set up. "You didn't do anything!" he accused. "I watched your hand. It didn't move."

Turning to him, Merry smiled. "Exactly," she said. "I didn't do anything. All I did was to relax my fingers enough for the string to do the work."

"Merry wants to talk to you," Scarlett was saying now, bringing Gabe back to the present. "Look, she's waving us over."

After carefully closing the book, Gabe put it safely back in his pocket and followed Scarlett over to the roughly carved wooden table that stood at the back of the oak tree, in the shade of its magnificent canopy.

Gabe noticed that Midge had something delicious bubbling in the cooking pot that hung, suspended from a branch, above the fire to one side of the table. His stomach growled in response.

Merry had a sheet of parchment spread out on the table in front of her and, glancing at it as he sat down opposite her, Gabe saw that it was a rough map. There were no words on the map, no place names or markers, just lines and small drawings.

"What is this?" he asked.

"Rothwell," said Merry, looking up from studying the sheet. "Gwyn's been working on it for weeks. This is the castle –" She pointed to a circle right at the heart of the town, well within the high stone walls that surrounded Rothwell.

"I've never been to Rothwell," Gabe said, "but I've seen it."

Merry frowned. "How have you seen it?" she asked.

"From the Abbey windows," said Gabe. "We're on top of the hill, looking down, so we get a good view of the town from above. Our dormitory looked right over this –" He indicated a large square at the bottom of the map. "It's the market square, I think."

Merry and Gwyn looked at each other. "It is," said Merry. "What else do you recognize?"

Gabe leaned over, feeling a slight breeze lift the damp hair at the nape of his neck. It was an unseasonably hot day and his heavy robe was uncomfortable. "I think this is the gatehouse," he said, pointing to a crosshatched rectangle set within the walls. "The road leads right to it and we'd often see travelers waiting there to be let in."

Gabe peered more closely at the map. "That's the cathedral," he said, pointing to a rectangle marked with a cross. "We hear their bells on Sunday, though they're not, I think, as loud as ours.

"I don't recognize that," Gabe continued, dropping his finger onto a thick, dark, snaking line that appeared to run behind the town walls down to the river beyond.

"That's because it's not there," said Gwyn with a smirk. "Well, not unless you know it's there."

Catching sight of Gabe's confused expression, Merry elbowed her sister. "It's a tunnel," she said. "It runs from the town to the river. Gwyn found it."

"But what's it for?" Gabe asked.

"We don't know," admitted Merry. "All we know is that it's the only way in and out of Rothwell apart from the gatehouse – and the tunnel doesn't require traveling papers."

Gabe sat back. He'd seen traveling papers before, of course – working in the guesthouse, part of his role had been to make sure that every person who requested a night's stay had permission from their Lord to be on the road.

"What is it you're planning to do?" he asked, his voice shaking a little.

"We're going to get our pa," said Merry, confidently. "We've been working on a plan for a long time, and now that we've got you . . ."

Gabe stared around at the four solemn faces looking at him. "What exactly is it that you think I can do for you?" he asked.

"Two things," said Merry, ignoring a warning glance from Gwyn. "Firstly, I want you to make some traveling papers for Scarlett here – calling her something else, of course."

Gabe nodded. Traveling papers took many forms, but he knew the information that was needed for them to pass.

"Secondly, I want you to accompany Scarlett to Rothwell tomorrow," Merry went on and this time Gabe felt Gwyn kick her sister under the table. "As part of the day's festivities, Lord Sherborne is allowing prisoners in the dungeon to receive their annual visit. I want you to go."

"Why me?" he asked. "Wouldn't it be better if you went – that way you could at least see him?"

"Because they're not looking for a couple," said Merry. "But if Gwyn and I go, they might suspect something. At the moment, they haven't connected us with the, er, incidents on the Rothwell Road and, if anything, seem to think that we're all boys." She broke off at Gwyn's loud hmmph.

"As far as the soldiers are concerned, Gwyn and I died the night that our pa was taken and we'd like to keep it that way," Merry repeated, frowning at her sister. "If you and Scarlett go in as a couple, you can make sure his cell door is open at the right time."

"And?" prompted Gabe, feeling there had to be more.

"And . . . act as lookouts for us," Merry went on. "Warn us if anything goes wrong."

"Warn you? Where will you be?" asked Gabe.

"We'll go in through the tunnel and come and get Pa," said Merry.

Gabe stared at the map. "Where exactly does the tunnel come out?" he asked.

"That's just it," said Merry. "As far as Gwyn can tell, it goes right up under the castle."

"As far as she can tell?" repeated Gabe.

"There's a locked door there, isn't there?" Gwyn said. "I didn't want to break the lock and show our hand. But I'm pretty sure it ends up under the castle – which is where Pa is."

"Pretty sure" didn't sound certain enough for Gabe, but Gwyn's fierce expression warned him against speaking.

"Won't Scarlett be recognized?" Gabe asked instead.

"Oh no," said Scarlett. "No one will know it's me. Just as no one will know it's you."

She fixed her blue eyes on him and Gabe shuddered. He got the feeling he wasn't going to like what she had in mind.

"Gabe," Merry said, drawing his attention back to her and the task at hand. "If you help us to do this, we'll help you."

"You've already helped me," Gabe said, "all of you. If it wasn't for you, I'd be in the castle dungeon right now."

He took a deep breath before continuing, almost unable to believe what he was saying. "I'll help. If you think I can do this, then I'll help."

Merry laughed. "Of course you can do it," she said. "Your part's easy! Well, once you've made the papers it is, anyway. All you have to do is do as you're told and keep your eyes and ears open."

Gabe nodded. He could do that. He was good at that. Isn't that what he'd been doing all his life in the Abbey – obeying, watching and learning?

"That's settled then," said Merry, dusting her hands together. "Tell Gwyn what you need to make the papers and she'll get it for you. We don't have much time."

"Why do we have to go tomorrow?" Gabe asked. "Is there a reason?"

"Where have you been?" asked Scarlett, aghast. "Haven't you heard the news?"

Gabe shook his head. "What news?"

"The Prince is coming," she said. "He traveled to Rothwell today to meet Lord Sherborne and tomorrow he's going to appear in the Royal Box at the Tournament."

"That's why we're going tomorrow," said Gwyn, grimly. "Everyone will be so busy staring at him that we'll go unnoticed."

But Gabe wasn't listening, deep in thought about the strange men in the velvet cloaks who had visited the Prior the night that Brother Benedict had disappeared. He felt for the book in his pocket, wondering about the timing of the Prior's sudden interest in it, and the Prince's visit. No royal had ever visited Rothwell before as far as Gabe could remember.

"When was it announced?" he asked. "That he was coming, I mean."

"The village criers were full of the news a few days ago," said Gwyn. "The day before we found you in the forest."

And yet not a word had been spoken about it at the Abbey, Gabe thought, before dismissing his own suspicions. Perhaps the Abbot had been meeting with the men in cloaks about the visit? Perhaps that's why he wasn't where he was supposed to be that night? Perhaps he was at this very moment in Rothwell preparing for the visit?

That must be it, Gabe thought, ignoring the tiny voice in his mind reminding him that the Prior had announced the Abbot to be ill.

"Anyway, plenty of time to talk about this later," said Merry, bringing him back to the table. "For now, let's get those papers done."

"Yes," said Scarlett, with a sunny smile. "And then it will be my turn to be creative."

Gabe had a very bad feeling that Scarlett's creativity had nothing to do with parchment and quills – and everything to do with him.

✥

"Your own mother wouldn't know you," said Scarlett with satisfaction.

"No," said Gabe, staring at himself in her tiny pocket mirror, trying to take in his new hair color. "She probably wouldn't – but then I don't think she would have known me before you started."

"Oh, I'm sorry," said Scarlett, clapping a hand over her mouth in horror. "I didn't think. It's just an expression."

Gabe managed a laugh. "It's all right," he said. "I'm used to it. Which is more than I can say for my hair."

The morning sun was only just peeping over the trees, but he'd already been up for hours, having been woken by Scarlett, who'd cut his hair, washed it in some foul-smelling liquid and then modestly turned her back as he'd struggled into the new clothes she'd given him.

"What do you want me to do with this?" Scarlett asked now, holding his faithful brown robe up as though it was diseased. "Throw it on the fire?"

Tearing his eyes from his reflection, Gabe glanced over at her. If he looked different with his brown hair dyed a strange yellow color, Scarlett was positively transformed. Her long golden hair was now almost black and she'd garbed herself in a ragged brown gown and flat shoes with a strap and buckle. A tattered head cloth and dirty face completed the picture. She looked as though she'd just stepped out of the fields.

Gabe looked down at his own clothes, wondering if they looked as strange as they felt. The rough linen lace-up tunic and loose, drawstring breeches he wore felt flimsy, and he missed the comforting swish of his robes around his ankles. Not that he would feel it in the boots he wore laced up to his calves, making his feet feel heavy and unwieldy. Who'd have thought he'd miss his sandals?

"I'll just leave it over here," he said now to Scarlett, taking the robe from her and clutching it to his chest. "I might need it again."

Her face softened. "Okay," she said, and he could hear the doubt in her voice. Scarlett didn't think he'd be needing his robe again any time soon.

"Right," she said. "We should be going. It's a fair walk to Rothwell and the others will be almost there."

Merry and Gwyn had left hours before, taking Midge with them for safety. Gabe could still see Gwyn's smirk at his miserable face as he sat, wrapped in only a coarse woolen blanket, the foul-smelling liquid with which Scarlett had dyed his hair dripping down his face and into his ears.

"You remember the signal?" Scarlett asked now, as she picked up the small basket of apples she intended to carry as part of her disguise. Hidden under the top two layers of fruit was the heavy knife that had been hanging on the wall and another smaller knife that Midge used for cooking.

Gabe whistled the melancholy five-note tune he'd heard in the woods that first day. "I do," he said to Scarlett. It was a melody that Merry and Gwyn's pa had taught them, and the little family had used it on hunting trips together.

"Good," said Scarlett. "Let's go."

Collecting a walking stick from beside the door, he remembered Merry's words as she'd handed it to him that morning before she'd left. "They're handy in a fight," Merry had said, demonstrating to Gabe how to sweep the stick low to knock the feet out from under an attacker, before swinging it high and smashing a pumpkin she'd set upon a tree branch.

Grasping the stick in one hand now, Gabe doubted he'd ever be able to use it on someone's head, but he had to admit that the solid wood in his hands did give him courage. Following Scarlett from the clearing into the gloom of the woods, he had a feeling he'd be needing every bit of courage he could muster.

"Remember, keep your head down," Scarlett whispered in Gabe's ear and he obliged, staring down at his feet as the long line of people waiting at the Rothwell Gate slowly trudged forward. Listening to the excited chatter of the people around him, he couldn't help but feel buoyed by the party atmosphere. Everyone in the line was here to see the Prince, to sell their wares and enjoy the festivities.

It had been a long time since Lord Sherborne had laid on a jousting tourney for his citizens – in fact, all the comments Gabe had heard on the Rothwell Road had supported his impression that it had been a long time since Lord Sherborne had done much at all for his people.

Gabe was realizing just how isolated his life in the Abbey had been. There, food was always plentiful, the atmosphere always peaceful and every day was much the same. It seemed that out in the fields and tumbledown cottages around Rothwell, life was hard.

The babble of voices washed over him and Gabe frowned, struck by a tiny, niggling worry. What was it? He listened harder, but there was nothing in particular in what people were talking about. What was it then?

Gabe looked more closely at the people surrounding him and Scarlett, but he could see nothing untoward there. Everyone was clad in the same rough tunics and gowns as they were, in shades of gray and brown and cream. Bright colors were for nobility and those who could afford them. No, it wasn't that. But there was a wrong chord somewhere and he needed to figure it out or he and Scarlett wouldn't get past the soldiers at the gate.

"What's the matter?" Scarlett whispered in his ear, her eyes looking down at the apples in her basket. "You look like you've smelled a rat."

As she spoke, the penny dropped. Her voice! All around Gabe, peasants were speaking with the rough accent of the region, drawing out their vowels, dropping their aitches. But Scarlett spoke like the lady that she was, all rounded sounds and an air of haughtiness that no peasant disguise would counteract.

"You can't speak," Gabe hissed under his breath at her. "They'll be on to you in seconds if you open your mouth. Give me your papers and leave any talking to me."

Scarlett's eyebrows nearly hit her hairline at the order, but they were nearing the front of the line now and so she said nothing. Swallowing hard against his nerves, Gabe took her traveling papers from her and folded them with his own.

"Next," said a brusque voice, and Gabe handed over the papers without looking up. Sweat dripped down his back as he heard the soldier rustling the vellum, seeming to take an inordinately long time to read the two short pages.

"From Lewes Hollow, are we?" the gruff voice asked, and Gabe peered up under his lashes to see a wrinkled face almost hidden by a stiff gray moustache.

"Aye," Gabe answered, staring back at his boots. He could hear Scarlett's quick breathing beside him and wanted to elbow her to calm down.

"Hmm," said the soldier, drawing out the sound.

Gabe said nothing, though his heart raced.

"Married, are we?" the soldier asked, and Gabe could hear the smirk in his voice.

"Aye," Gabe answered.

"Typical peasants," the soldier said with a ribald laugh, nudging the armored man beside him. "Start 'em young to keep the worker numbers up. She's probably your cousin 'n' all." The other soldier laughed, the movement making his sword clank against his metal-clad leg.

Gabe blushed but said nothing, knowing that the less he spoke the better.

"Well, I'll let you have your fun today," the soldier said, and he clipped the corners of the papers Gabe had written out so carefully the night before. "Lord knows you probably don't have much of it. Just be sure to steer clear of the Royal party. They don't need to see the likes of you."

With that, he ushered them through the gate and Scarlett grabbed Gabe's hand, pulling him inside and out of the push of people walking up the cobbled street and into a quiet spot in the shadow of the great stone wall that encircled Rothwell.

"What a mean man," Gabe said, anger making his face hot. "Why did he speak to us like that? He doesn't even know us."

"His type don't need to know us to make judgements," Scarlett said. "Only a few months ago, I would have been the same as him. Have you never judged a person by their appearance or what you may have heard about people like him or her?"

Gabe thought. "At the Abbey we're taught to treat everyone as equal," he said. "We all dressed the same, we all talked about the same things, none of us had more than anyone else."

"And you never looked down upon a poor man who arrived at the guesthouse in rags and without shoes?" she asked.

"No," Gabe answered. "All our guests were housed in the same room, fed the same food. If a man had no shoes, we tried to find him some."

Scarlett sighed. "It's worse than I thought," she said. "I fear that you will find life out here even more difficult than I imagined."

Gabe managed a smile at her concern. "I'm told that I am a fast learner," he said.

"Well," said Scarlett, hitching her basket higher on her hip, "lessons start today and you're just going to have to keep up."

With that, she turned and stepped back into the flow of humanity jostling its way up the street in the direction, from what Gabe remembered, of the Green, situated to one side of the castle. Looking up as he followed her, Gabe could see the pointed turrets of the castle rising high above the rooflines of the narrow stone townhouses that lined each side of the street. Jaunty flags of red and purple flew from the battlements that encircled each rounded corner.

If all had gone to plan, Merry, Gwyn and Midge were deep below the streets, making their way to the locked door that stood between them and the girls' father. Remembering his role, Gabe resolved to keep his eyes and ears open for the slightest hint of trouble as he and Scarlett made their way to the castle doors.

Stepping into the town square, Gabe noticed one entire wall plastered in the "pictures" that Gwyn had warned him about, and he swallowed hard when he recognized a fading painting of Scarlett's face staring out at him, with the word MISSING underneath.

He nudged her and she gasped, dragging him away, but not before he caught a glimpse of a fresh picture not far from Scarlett's. Gabe hissed under his breath when he saw the word THIEF below his own face.

Walking quickly now towards the dungeon entrance, keeping his eyes focused on the cobbled street, Gabe could only hope this went as smoothly as Merry seemed certain it would – because otherwise he didn't know how they'd all get out of here again.

CHAPTER EIGHT

It was the smell that nearly brought Gabe undone. The stench of sweat and urine and despair that rose up the stairs grew stronger the deeper down into the dungeons they went, nearly knocking him over by the time they reached the gloomy iron gate at the bottom.

"Papers," demanded a wizened man at the door, and Gabe handed them over, wishing he could hold his nose with his other hand.

"Who're you here for?" the little man demanded.

Gabe swallowed, realizing he didn't even know Merry's pa's name – nor, he realized, what crime the man had been arrested for. He'd taken the girls at face value when they'd said he wasn't guilty, mostly because Merry and Gwyn seemed so *honest*, despite their way of life. But, really, what would he know?

As his conversation with Scarlett had shown him, what he didn't know about people would fill the secret book, which he'd left behind, tucked into a small hollow high in the branches of the oak tree. Midge had left Albert tethered nearby, his hood in place to keep him quiet.

"Ralf Hodges," Scarlett mumbled and Gabe noted with relief that she'd made an effort to disguise her refined accent.

"The poacher?" The man's wrinkled face creased even further. "Make the most of it. He'll not be with us much longer."

There was a small silence whilst Gabe and the man waited for Scarlett to respond, but she said nothing. Gabe took in the word "poacher" and wondered about Ralf Hodges's extended stay in the dungeon. Poaching was against the law and everyone knew it, but Gabe also knew from his time in the Abbey kitchens that an occasional grouse or piece of wild boar made its way out of the forest.

Brother Primus, who ran the guesthouse, sometimes accepted these offerings instead of payment for a night's accommodation and brought them down to the kitchen with a cheeky smile on his face. "Another poor animal died of natural causes on the Rothwell Road," he'd say.

Scarlett said nothing to defend her uncle. The man went on, still riffling through their papers.

"Nothing to say? That'd be right. Neither has he. But everyone knows what he did – putting an arrow in the King's stag? What was he thinking?"

The man seemed genuinely perplexed and Gabe could understand it. Even *he'd* heard of the King's stag, most noble and sacred beast in the entire forest. If it had come to harm at Ralf Hodges's hands, then . . . Gabe gulped. Merry and Gwyn's pa was destined to die.

"Anyway," the man at the gate said, holding out their papers, "make the most of your visit today. It will be your last. It's been decided he'll be walking on air before year's end. Last door on the left – Harald will open the cell."

Scarlett made a sound in her throat like she was swallowing a sob and Gabe took the papers and ushered her through the door.

"What does he mean, walking on air?" Gabe whispered as they made their way down the dark, dank corridor, following the hulking guard. His shoulder brushed against the damp stone wall as they passed and he shivered, feeling the wet patch bloom on his tunic.

"They're going to hang him," Scarlett sighed. "Every year Lord Sherborne hangs three prisoners at Winterfest as a warning for the following year."

Gabe was aghast. "Do the girls know?"

"I don't know," Scarlett said, shaking her head. "But it means we have to succeed today – this is the last visiting day before Winterfest. We won't get the cell door open again."

"Hodges!" said Harald, running his sword along the bars inset into the door of the cell at the farthest end of the corridor, making a clanking sound loud enough to wake the dead. "Someone to see you."

Harald pulled a large ring of keys from the belt on his hip and made a great show of selecting one, jangling the others as he did so. Gabe looked around, wondering just how Gwyn intended to get herself and the other girls in here. He could see no sign of a door anywhere in the gloomy corridor.

Now Harald was opening the solid timber door, which swung open with a long creak. There was no sound of movement within.

"Ten minutes," said Harald, turning to Gabe and Scarlett with a smirk. "I'll be back." He pushed past them and strode off down the corridor, his footsteps heavy on the stone floor.

"What do we do now?" Gabe whispered.

"Go in, of course," said Scarlett, "and hope the others get here soon."

With that, she plastered on a smile and stepped into the cell, Gabe following so close behind that when she stopped dead in front of him, he ran up the back of her.

"What's wrong?" he asked. "Why have you stopped?"

"Look!" she said, pointing to the corner.

Eyes adjusting to the darkness in the cell, which was lit only by a single narrow vertical slit cut into the stone high up the wall, Gabe could make out an older man slumped against the wall. His gray hair hung down below his shoulders, as did his thick gray beard. Ralf Hodges did not appear to be weathering his incarceration well.

To Gabe's surprise, however, there was another figure beside Ralf, getting warily to his feet, eyeing them both with suspicion. He stepped closer and Gabe could see that it was a boy of about sixteen, tall and dark, and, judging by his healthy appearance, new to dungeon life.

"Who are you?" the boy asked, imperiously. "What do you want? Are you here to rescue me?"

Scarlett laughed. "You? Why would we be here to rescue you? We are here to see Ralf Hodges."

Ignoring the boy's spluttered response, Scarlett rushed over to her uncle, taking out a water skin that she'd put in her basket with the apples and holding it to his lips. Gabe could see her whispering to him, but couldn't make out what was said.

"You have to get me out of here," the boy was saying to Gabe. "I'm —" He got no further, instead staring open-mouthed over Gabe's shoulder. "Who are you?" the boy said. "Where did you come from?"

Gabe turned to see Gwyn, Midge and Merry all sliding silently into the cell and arranging themselves along the wall behind the door, where they wouldn't be seen should anyone glance casually inside.

"I know you, don't I?" asked Merry, looking curiously at the boy. "You live down by the mill. What's he doing here?" She turned her last question to Gabe.

"I don't know," Gabe said with a grimace.

"I'm trying to tell you," said the boy. "I'm —"

"Shh," said Gwyn, and everyone stilled, listening to the beat of heavy footsteps down the corridor.

"Everything all right in there?" came the gruff voice of Harald the guard, fast approaching.

Gwyn, Midge and Merry slid farther behind the door, but Gabe knew they'd be spotted as soon as the guard came into the cell. Almost without thinking, Gabe stepped outside.

"All's well," Gabe said to the man, as cheerfully as he could. "My, er, wife is just a bit upset at seeing, er, Ralf."

"Caterwauling, is she?" Harald asked, stopping in his tracks. "I hate caterwauling women. I'd rather they shouted than cried."

Gabe managed a smile. "Er, yes," he said, though he had no idea what caterwauling was. "Caterwauling. So much caterwauling."

"Right, well, I'll leave you to deal with that," Harald said, turning and retreating back to the gate. "You've got five more minutes then you'll need to bring her out."

Gabe nodded and stepped back into the cell, wondering how they were going to pull this off. Five minutes wasn't enough time for anything.

As soon as Harald was gone, Merry and Gwyn moved to their father, trying to pull him to his feet.

"Pa," Merry whispered urgently, "it's me. We have to go."

Ralf looked at her, dazed. "Merry?" he croaked. "My Merry?"

"Me too," Gwyn said, holding her pa's hand, her white hair seeming to glow in the dim cell. "Stand up, Pa, we have to go."

But he was shaking his head, looking up at them. "My girls," he whispered. "I thought I'd never see you again."

"We've come to take you home," Merry said, kneeling down beside him, and Gabe could hear the tears in her voice.

But again, Ralf shook his head. "No, love," he said. "I can't go. Can't walk, too weak. We'd all be caught."

Now Gwyn was kneeling too, clutching her father's arm. "I've found a way, Pa, a good way."

He turned to look at her, and Gabe saw all the love in the world in his face. "Ah, Gwynnie my girl, I'm sure you have. If anyone could, it's you. But I can't do it. My legs . . ."

They all looked down at his legs, stretched out on the floor before him and Gabe noticed for the first time the green and yellow pus that streaked the man's breeches.

"Pa!" Merry said, horrified. "What have they done to you?"

"I'm all right, Merry girl," Ralf said. "Just a bit sore from a run-in with a guard a few weeks ago, but –"

"We'll carry you," Merry said, fiercely. "There are five of us. We can –"

"No, love," said Ralf, and Gabe could hear the weakness and fatigue in his voice, but also that underlying steel that his oldest daughter had inherited. "You go. Kiss me quick and go. We'll find another way, another day."

"But –" Gabe and Scarlett spoke at once, and Gabe knew that she was thinking about Winterfest, as he was.

"No buts," said Ralf, glaring at both of them. "I don't know who you are," Ralf went on, addressing Gabe, "but this is family business." Gabe nodded, feeling sick, realizing that Ralf didn't want the girls to know about the hanging. There was no way that the man was going to be able to leave with them, and no way the girls would go without him if they knew it would be the last time they'd see him.

"Take him instead," Ralf said, pointing at the boy who was standing silently by the door.

"Pa!" said Merry, sounding as though she was in agony. "No!"

"Yes, Merry," said Ralf, and Gabe again heard the steel. "I'm your father and I want you to take him."

"Why?" asked Gwyn with a frown. "Why should we? We came to get you."

Her father's face softened. "Ah Gwynnie, because it's the right thing to do," said Ralf. "Trust me."

"We have to go," said Merry, sadly. "There can't be much time left. Oh, Pa!"

Merry threw her arms around her father's neck, burying her face in his shirt, while Gwyn did the same on the other side. They couldn't see it, but Gabe didn't miss the deep sadness on Ralf Hodges's face as he patted their backs.

"There, there," he said. "I'll be better soon and we can try again. I know my Gwyn – if you got in this time, you can get in again."

Gwyn sat up, nodding fiercely. "We'll come back for you, Pa. As soon as we can."

"Right, off with you then," said Ralf, waving weakly in the direction of the door. "Keep safe." The way he said it made Gabe think that these were words he'd used many times before with his girls.

"Anyone coming?" Merry asked, and Midge stuck her head out the door to check the corridor.

"No," she reported, but Gabe knew that time was ticking down. Harald wouldn't be far away.

With one last fierce hug for her father, Merry stood. "Let's go," she said. "Lead the way, Gwyn."

Gwyn squeezed Ralf's hand and turned to face them. Gabe saw that the emotion of just moments ago was gone, replaced by her usual cold, distant expression.

"You follow me, you don't say a word," Gwyn said, looking at Gabe, Scarlett and the stranger.

"But –" said the boy.

"Not. One. Word," Gwyn said, interrupting him. "Follow."

With that, she was out the door and into the gloomy corridor.

"Go," said Merry. "Midge and I will be behind you."

So Gabe went, with Scarlett and the strange boy at his heels. Out in the corridor, Gabe was surprised to find that Gwyn had turned left and was standing in a corner of the shallow alcove that formed the end of the corridor.

"What are you doing?" he asked. "That's not the way out."

"It's my way out," Gwyn said and, bending down, shoved her fingers into a crack that had formed between the bricks in the right-hand joint of the alcove. To Gabe's surprise, a small portion of the stone wall began to move.

"Help me," she said, looking up at him. "It's easier to push it from the other side, but it's heavy."

Leaning over her, with the others watching on, Gabe slid his fingers into the wider crack she'd created and pulled as hard as he could with his fingertips. A small section of the wall began opening outward, and Gabe admired the clever construction that had allowed the brickwork to act as a hinge.

"In you go," said Gwyn, ushering him forward. "You'll need to get on your stomach."

Bending low, Gabe wriggled through the opening into the yawning darkness beyond. To his surprise, it opened up just half a body length inside, and he was able to pull himself out into a tunnel that, feeling about him, he determined was just taller than his head and as wide as two people.

"Move forward," came a voice behind him, and Gabe jumped out of the way, realizing that he was blocking the path of the strange boy.

Within moments, he could hear the girls tumbling through the door and into the tunnel. As they did so, the door was shut behind them, taking with it the tiny bit of light that had been present.

"I've locked the door from this side," Gwyn whispered, joining them. "Now we need to move. I don't know who knows about this tunnel and who doesn't, but the fact that you've disappeared with *him* means that everyone will be searching."

They'd have been searching for us if we'd disappeared with your pa too, thought Gabe, but he bit back the words on his lips. No point in starting a fight while they were all stuck in a tunnel.

He felt Gwyn slide down the wall past the others, taking her position at the head of the line. "Drop the basket, Scarlett," Gwyn said as she passed her cousin. "Leave the apples but keep the knives – one for you and one for Sandals."

"What about me?" protested the strange boy, as muffled shouts and banging filtered through the thick wall behind them.

"You don't get a weapon until we know who you are," came Merry's determined whisper. "And right now we don't have time for introductions. Stay close, everyone."

Gabe imagined the confusion in the cell they'd just left, where, to Harald, it would look as though he and Scarlett had simply vanished into thin air, taking the other boy with them. He wondered if Merry and Gwyn were thinking of their pa, who would surely bear some of the brunt of the boy's disappearance.

Gabe could only hope Ralf's dazed condition protected him a little – it wouldn't take much for him to feign complete bewilderment, given the state of him. With any luck, he'd be quick enough to say that he'd never seen either Scarlett or Gabe in his life and that the pair of them must be tied in some way to the other boy.

Gabe shuddered. He'd heard terrible stories of what went on in the castle dungeons, and could only hope that he and the girls hadn't caused Ralf Hodges any further harm.

Feeling sick to his stomach, Gabe concentrated on putting one foot in front of the other and not falling over in the darkness. Gwyn was setting a cracking pace and he didn't want to give her any reason to call him out. Gabe had to admit that running was certainly easier without his long robes, and the stout boots might be heavier, but they were keeping his feet dry as they splashed through trickles of who-knew-what underfoot.

All Gabe could hear was the footsteps of the group fleeing with him, and the harshness of their breathing as they toiled through the never-ending darkness. The tunnel twisted and turned to such a degree that Gabe kept bashing into walls, taken by surprise with each new direction.

Gwyn, of course, had no such trouble and Gabe wondered if she could see in the dark like a cat. He filed it away in his mind. The evidence for her being a faerie was mounting.

The one bright side was that, so far, there was no sign that anyone had discovered the door in the wall. The muffled shouts and banging noises had faded as soon as they'd gone deeper into the tunnel and, whilst Gwyn did stop occasionally to listen, shushing them all, they could hear no sound up ahead.

After what felt like an age, Gwyn stopped again, this time so suddenly that Gabe ran up the back of her, treading on the heel of her boot, causing her to curse viciously under her breath.

"Sorry," he whispered, knowing that she wasn't even listening to him, distracted by the pale light filtering in to the tunnel in this spot.

Looking up, Gabe saw a narrow shaft that stretched high above them, a tiny spot of light at its very top. "Shh!" she said, and they all obediently stood as still and silently as possible, even the new boy, who seemed to have realized quickly that Gwyn wasn't to be messed with.

Moments ticked by, and Gabe could hear his heartbeat racing and a rushing in his ears as the silence seemed to grow louder.

"What is it?" Merry finally asked her sister in a low voice.

"Entrance is not far," Gwyn whispered. "I'll just go ahead and check that all is well."

"Did you hear something?" Merry asked.

"I hear nothing," said Gwyn. "And that's what worries me."

Gabe frowned in the darkness, wondering what Gwyn meant, but she'd gone, running so lightly down the tunnel that he wondered if she was actually flying. The other five waited in the darkness, saying nothing. Gabe adjusted his tunic, pulling the fabric away from his sweating neck and taking shallow breaths. He couldn't wait to get out of the hot, airless tunnel and see the sky again.

How must Ralf Hodges feel after being in his dungeon cell for two years, his only fresh air that which found its way through the narrow slit in the wall? Gabe's heart sank as he realized the true ramifications of having left Ralf behind, and he hoped against hope that it would be Scarlett who would tell her cousins about Winterfest. He did not envy the bearer of such news.

So lost in his dark thoughts was he that he nearly hit his head on the tunnel roof when Gwyn silently appeared beside him. "Soldiers," she said. "Three of them poking around in the woods down by the river. That's why the birds aren't singing."

Gabe took in the fact that the "nothing" that she'd heard was the lack of birdsong.

"Are they watching the tunnel entrance?" Merry whispered.

"Don't think they know it's there," said Gwyn, and Gabe frowned, wondering how they could miss an entrance as tall and wide as this.

"What will we do?" asked Scarlett.

"Merry and I will go first," said Gwyn, "and lead them away. You follow with Midge and *them.*"

"I say —" said the strange boy.

"No," said Gwyn, "you don't say. If you want to get out of here, you do as I *say.*"

The boy muttered something under his breath, but said no more. Gabe was more than happy to put himself in Gwyn's hands again — it had worked out for him so far.

"Okay," Gwyn said. "After we leave, you sing three versus of 'Once a Fair Maiden' — quietly mind — and then follow. Not before. Head straight for the end of the tunnel, get yourself out, and get behind the tallest elm on the left and wait for me. Don't look left or right, don't decide you'll hide elsewhere, just do as you're told and we'll all get home safe."

"Got it," said Midge and Scarlett, and Gabe could hear the trust in their voices.

"What will you do?" Gabe asked, his curiosity getting the better of him. "You're not going to kill anyone are you?"

Merry chuckled. "Don't worry, Gabe, your soul is safe with us. We're just going to lead them on a little chase."

"We'll need to be quick," Gwyn told her sister. "Get your longbow and run."

"Aye, aye," said Merry, and Gabe felt the whistle of air as she pretended to salute Gwyn. He wondered how she could joke at a time like this.

"Start singing," said Gwyn, and Gabe felt Merry push past him as she followed her sister towards the entrance of the tunnel.

"Wait a minute," said the strange boy. "Why are we singing?"

Scarlett sighed. "To mark time, of course," she said, as though speaking to a small child.

There was a pause. "Why not just count?" asked the boy, and Gabe stared at him in the dark, wondering where a boy who lived beside a mill had learned to count.

"What's your name?" asked Scarlett, suspiciously.

"Edward," said the boy and, for the first time, Gabe heard uncertainty in his tone.

"Well, Eddie," said Scarlett, "it's lovely that you can count, but some of us can't, so we sing instead, all right?"

Without waiting for a response, she launched quietly into the chorus of "Once a Fair Maiden," Midge joining in immediately.

Once a Fair Maiden went a-walking, tirralee,
Beside the River Bonnie she walked, did she,
A rose she wore at her throat, from me,
But in her heart was another.

So captivated by the plaintive beauty of Scarlett's singing was Gabe that he was shocked when he felt a sharp elbow in his ribs.

"Sing," hissed Midge.

Joining in on the second chorus, Gabe smiled. He loved to sing in the Abbey choir and found himself adding a descant harmony to Scarlett's soprano. Midge stopped singing as the two of them continued into the third chorus and Gabe found he had chills crawling over his skin at the sound of their blended voices in the dark.

"*Posblits!*" exclaimed Midge, "I'm going to tell Merry you two can sing – maybe you can make some money at Winterfest!"

Gabe frowned, not sure what the link between singing and Winterfest might be. The sobering mention of Ralf Hodges's hanging date also had the effect of focusing his mind on the task at hand. "We're not here to sing," he reminded the others. "We have to go."

Not waiting for a response, Gabe turned to face the direction that Merry and Gwyn had gone and, taking a deep breath, pressed forward into the dark. He had no idea what was awaiting him at the end of the tunnel, but he thought that not obeying Gwyn's instructions might lead to a worse fate . . .

"I won't fit through that!" Eddie spoke the words that Gabe was thinking. They were staring at a hole in the wall that seemed not much larger than Gabe's head.

"Surely this isn't the entrance?" asked Scarlett.

"It is," confirmed Midge. "Now you can see why it's remained so hidden."

"What could this tunnel possibly be used for?" asked Gabe, looking around him in the weak light. The stones in the tunnel wall were worn down to a smooth finish and he reached out to stroke the mossy surface. "Wait," he said, thinking about the map that Gwyn had shown him. "The mouth is close to the river. Do you think it's for water?"

The others stared at him.

"Yes," Gabe went on slowly, thinking about the shaft they'd seen farther up the tunnel. "I think it's used for water when the town is under siege. They can bring it up from the river and draw it up through a well."

"They flood the tunnel?" Eddie asked. "How?"

"I don't know," Gabe admitted, "but it makes sense."

"This is all very exciting," said Scarlett, in tones suggesting that it was not at all exciting, "but it's time to get out. Which means we need to slide through that hole."

"What if we get stuck?" asked Eddie, horrified.

"For that reason, you can go last because you're the biggest," decreed Scarlett. "Midge first, then me, then Gabe, then you."

Gabe swallowed, knowing that the last people out of the entrance had the most chance of being noticed, but he nodded.

"Go, Midgey," said Scarlett, and the little girl slid headfirst into the narrow opening, her arms leading the way to make herself as small as possible.

Scarlett went next, removing her bonnet, and wrapping her gown tightly around herself to try to reduce its bulk. Even so, she only just fitted into the opening and it took several minutes of frantic wriggling before her feet disappeared and the light filtered back through the opening.

"I don't think I'm going to make it," whispered Eddie. "I'm too big."

Looking at the boy's pale, trembling face, Gabe felt sorry for him. He had no idea what Eddie had done to end up in that cell with Ralf Hodges, but he knew that if he were Eddie, he'd do anything to ensure he didn't end up back in there.

"I'll tell you what," Gabe said with a sigh, "you go next – that way I can push you from behind if you get stuck."

"Oh, would you?" said Eddie, and Gabe frowned, suddenly realizing that the boy spoke more like Scarlett than like Merry and Gwyn. "I confess I've never done anything like this before."

"Neither have I," admitted Gabe. "But we don't have time to talk about it. You know what to do once you're through?"

"Turn left, tallest elm," said Eddie, exhaling loudly.

"In you go then."

Eddie put his hands through the opening and paused, muttering under his breath.

"What are you doing?" asked Gabe, impatiently. "We don't have all day."

"Praying," said Eddie. "It seems like a good idea."

With that, he pushed his arms through the opening, diving headfirst after them. Gabe winced, watching Eddie's shoulders hit the outer edges of the narrow space, and the other boy twisted and turned to get them in, his legs kicking furiously as his body was swallowed up by the stones.

At first, Eddie seemed to be making decent, if slow, progress as though he were being eaten at a leisurely pace. But then he stopped and the kicking of his legs became more frenzied. Trying not to get a foot in the face, Gabe grabbed Eddie's right leg.

"Stop kicking!" he hissed, and the legs stilled, allowing Gabe to position himself at the ankles. Holding Eddie's legs straight, in line with the bottom of the opening, Gabe bent low and pushed as hard as he could, ignoring Eddie's grunts of pain.

"Shh," said Gabe, worried that the strange noises would attract the attention of anyone outside.

Feeling sweat dripping down his face, Gabe stopped for a moment before renewing his efforts and pushing again. The legs inched forward, and he could feel Eddie twisting and turning, trying to move his shoulders. Gabe could only hope that Eddie's head wasn't hanging out of the entrance.

Breathing hard, Gabe stopped again, wondering if Scarlett's prophecy was going to come true. Would Eddie be stuck in the narrow opening forever? Which meant, Gabe realized, swallowing, that Gabe would be stuck in the tunnel behind him forever – or until the guards in the dungeon above found the hidden door to the tunnel and came stomping down here to get him.

Taking two steps back, Gabe dropped his shoulder and ran forward to give Eddie's legs an almighty shove. At first he felt as though it wasn't going to work, that his best efforts would amount to nothing. But, suddenly, like a cork from a bottle, Eddie slithered out of the opening with a sharp cry and a loud thump.

Gabe half inserted his head into the opening, trying to see beyond the bright daylight at the entrance.

"Eddie?" he whispered.

He heard nothing but rustling, followed by the sound of scrambling feet. Gabe stilled, waiting, but there was no more. He could feel a light breeze blowing in through the opening, tickling his nostrils. Suddenly, Gabe wanted nothing more than to be out there in the sunshine.

Backing up slightly, Gabe pushed his arms into the opening ahead of him, feeling the smoothness of the stones, still warm from Eddie's body. With a wriggle, he managed to get his arms and head inside and, turning slightly and slumping, pushed off with his feet and slid his shoulders in. It was a snug fit, but he was happy to realize that he had a small amount of room to squirm – which was more than Eddie had had.

Kicking his legs behind him, Gabe continued to writhe his way through the opening, feeling the hard stone bruising his hips, sweat trickling down his back. Once, he cracked his shin savagely on the edge of the opening and had to bite back a yelp of pain, but mostly he concentrated on using small movements to wriggle his way towards the light.

Just when he thought he was going to be entombed in rock forever, Gabe felt his hands pop through the hole at the entrance. Grasping the outside edge of the opening, he pulled as hard as he could in the confined space, shooting forward until he was blinded by brilliant light. His head was free!

Buoyed by his success, he reached down as far as he could and pushed hard against the wall, using the force to lever his shoulders through the opening, almost whooping with joy as he slithered out to land in an undignified heap in the dirt. Looking up, Gabe realized that the tunnel opening was about half a man's body height off the ground and, fortunately for him, well disguised behind a wall of sprawling hazel trees.

"Are you going to lie there all day?" came Gwyn's amused voice.

Scrambling to his feet, Gabe stared around but couldn't see her. "How do you do it?" he asked, the words falling unbidden from his lips.

"Do what?" she asked.

"Be everywhere and nowhere," he said.

She laughed, stepping out from the shrubbery beside him. "Practice," she said. "Pa's taken me hunting with him since I was a bairn. You learn to move like the animals move."

She paused, appearing to sniff the air. "Speaking of which," she said, "we have to go. You've taken too long. Merry has led the soldiers away, but I don't know how long they'll chase."

With that she was gone again, and he could do nothing but follow the quivering leaves she left in her wake, running towards the large elm on the left.

But when they got there, the others had gone.

"Where are they?" asked Gabe.

"I sent them on along," said Gwyn. "The safest thing for us to do is to follow the woods, steering clear of the Rothwell Road. Midge knows and Merry will loop back to meet them. They'll wait for us near the Abbey."

He frowned, following her as she picked her way through the trees via a path that only she seemed to be able to see. "Why the Abbey?" he asked.

"We're going to drop that boy off there," said Gwyn. "He can ask for sanctuary. He'll be safe."

"Isn't he safe with us?" asked Gabe.

"We don't need another mouth to feed," said Gwyn, shortly. "Particularly one we don't know."

"You didn't know me until a few days ago," reasoned Gabe.

"No," said Gwyn, "but for some reason Merry's taken a liking to you and so you stay."

Her tone suggested that if it was up to Gwyn, he'd have been wandering around in the woods by himself. "Anyway," she continued. "No talking now – we're skirting the back of the town."

So deep in the trees were they that Gabe hadn't even realized the walls of Rothwell were looming above them.

He wondered what was going on inside them, what sort of reaction there'd been to their disappearance.

He could only hope that nobody would miss Eddie too much.

Crouched in a hedgerow, Gabe listened to the silence and despaired. Beside him, Gwyn shifted ever so slightly, barely rustling the dense branches around them, before whistling the five-note melody for the third time.

Once again, there was no sound.

"They must be here," Gwyn muttered. "Merry left ages ago." She parted the leaves in front of her, giving her a better view of the road that ran alongside the Abbey. The hedgerow in which they hid was perfectly positioned to allow her to see the Abbey entrance.

Gabe rubbed his arm where a branch poked into his thick linen shirt. "Maybe they ran into trouble," he whispered.

"Merry never runs into trouble unless she wants to," Gwyn said.

But Merry is not alone.

Before Gabe could respond, Gwyn nudged him. "Horses," was all she said, moving swiftly to close the gap in the leaves, once again shrouding them both in greenery. Moments later, Gabe heard the thudding of hooves on the road.

"Don't move," Gwyn hissed under her breath and Gabe concentrated on keeping still. Within seconds, his nose began to wrinkle against the strong scent of the box leaves. Reaching up as slowly and as subtly as possible, he surreptitiously tried to block his nose against the smell, which reminded him of the scent cats used to mark their territory.

"Don't. Move."

Sliding his hand back down his side, Gabe tried to think about something else. Anything else, but the maddening little tickle, right on the end of his nose, continued to annoy him. It was as though little bugs had crawled under his skin.

Clenching his teeth, Gabe started counting backward silently – at which point a tiny spot on the top of his head also started to itch.

Before he could start to wonder if he was coming down with some kind of bramble-induced pox, Gwyn nudged him. "Look," she said, nodding almost imperceptibly in the direction of the Abbey doors, which, Gabe saw through the leaves, were creaking open.

Shrinking down into the brambles, Gabe watched in horror as Prior Dismas emerged, surrounded by Damman and four other Brothers wearing their cowls up over their heads so that their faces couldn't be seen, though surely the largest one was Brophy.

What was going on?

The question was answered moments later as an enormous black horse galloped up, skidding to a halt in a fever of lather and snorting, just a few feet from where the Prior and his henchmen – for Gabe could now not think of them any other way – were standing.

"Where is he?" demanded the large man sitting astride the horse. He was dressed all in black, from his boots to his cloak, and his hair was the same color, albeit with one wide streak of gray that ran down the back of his head.

"He is safe," said the Prior, a small, smug smirk playing about his mouth.

"Is he here?" the man asked.

"Of course not," snapped the Prior. "He's exactly where you told me to put him."

"Then he is NOT safe," roared the man, "unless it was *you* who removed him from the castle dungeon this afternoon!"

Even from across the road, Gabe could see the color drain from Prior Dismas's face and he felt no pity as the smile wilted. The man could only be speaking about Eddie, unless another prisoner had escaped that day. Gabe tried to imagine what link there could be between the Prior and the scruffy boy, but his mind was blank.

"What will you do?" asked the Prior, licking his thin lips.

"SEARCH FOR HIM, of course!" shouted the man. "As will you. Round up these silent specters and get to it.

Ronan of Feldham and my men are searching the forest as we speak. I WANT HIM BACK – at any cost. All our lives depend on it."

With that, the man pulled hard on his reins, the huge horse rearing up under him and turning on its hind legs. As it crashed to the ground, pawing the earth, the man turned back to the motionless Prior. "NOW!" he shouted, and galloped away at full speed.

Gabe ducked down farther into the hedge under a shower of dirt and rocks thrown up by the horse's huge hooves as it passed.

He looked up again to see the Prior fleeing back inside the Abbey, Damman and the other Brothers at his heels.

Beside him, Gwyn stirred and Gabe realized that she had not so much as twitched during the entire exchange.

"Are they talking about Eddie?" he whispered.

"We need to get back to the oak," she said, though she nodded. "Merry will make her way there. That's the rule."

"What's going on?" Gabe asked, almost to himself.

"I don't know," she admitted, "but I don't like it."

CHAPTER NINE

"It looks quiet," said Gabe, peering out through the thorns that surrounded him. He was heartily sick of sitting in shrubs and wanted nothing more than to cross the silent, sunny clearing in front of them and get inside the oak tree, make sure his book was safe, and to try to make sense of the day he'd just survived.

"It's too quiet," said Gwyn, echoing her words from outside the Abbey. Their flight through the forest had been swift and Gabe had concentrated on keeping the girl in sight as she'd flitted from tree to tree, pausing to listen and sniff the air, before moving forward. It had taken them twice as long to travel to the oak tree as it had the night they'd visited the Abbey but they'd run into no one along the way.

Once or twice, Gabe had heard tramping and rustling nearby or shouts in the distance, but Gwyn had quickly changed direction to avoid the searchers. At one point, she'd even insisted Gabe walk *in* a creek, with water splashing over the top of his sturdy boots and sloshing about inside them.

"Why are we doing this?" he'd asked her through gritted teeth.

"Dogs," was all she said, and even as she spoke he heard a faint howl on the breeze.

"Where are they?" Gwyn muttered now. "They should be here."

Gabe was about to suggest that they go and make sure the others weren't simply tucked up inside the oak, when Gwyn put a hand on his shoulder. As he closed his mouth, he heard voices nearby and the cracking sound of someone pushing through the brambles.

"What do we do?" he whispered to Gwyn.

"Stay still," she said, barely audible. "Everything's inside so it's just a tree to anyone but us."

Sure enough, Gabe watched dry mouthed as two men dressed in the livery of Lord Sherborne finally managed to extricate themselves from the thorny branches and fell into the clearing.

"That's it!" said the taller one, a thickset man with a ginger beard. "I've had enough of this. We don't even know who we're looking for."

The other man, bald and slight, looked about the clearing. "Well, there's no one here, that's for sure."

"Good," said the tall man, flopping down on the grass. "Wake me in an hour or so. We'll go back and tell Ronan we saw no one."

"Come on, Dan," said the bald man, looking nervous. "We'll pay the piper if he finds us here."

"He won't find us," murmured Dan, eyes closed. "No one will find us. Just as we'll find no one. Because *there's no one to find.*"

The bald man sat heavily beside him. "I hate the woods," he said. "They're itchy and scratchy and full of potholes and foxes."

Dan laughed without opening his eyes. "Too right. Give me a dark moldy tavern any day. All this fresh air can't be good for a man."

There was a short silence and Gabe wondered if Dan had fallen asleep. But then he spoke again.

"What do you reckon he really wants, Hal?"

"Who? Ronan?" asked Hal, who was now lying beside his friend on the grass.

Dan grunted.

"I don't know," his friend answered. "It's an awful lot of trouble for one young thief. Hey – I know. Maybe he stole the crown jewels!" He guffawed at his own joke.

"Yeah, and I'm the King of Alban," hooted Dan.

At that, the two stopped talking and soon the clearing was full of the loud, rhythmic sound of their snoring.

"What do we do now?" Gabe asked, looking at Gwyn.

She chewed her lip thoughtfully. "We wait," she decided. "Merry will come here when she's able. If we go looking for her, we might miss her – or run into more of them!" Gwyn nodded in the direction of the sleeping soldiers.

"And *them?*" he asked, also nodding at Hal and Dan.

"As much as it pains me, it's best to let them sleep it off and then go," sighed Gwyn. "I'd like to help them on their way at the point of a knife, but that would draw too much attention to us. We'll wait."

Gabe shifted position, stretching his wet boots out in front of him, creating a hollow in the brambles for his feet. "How long will it take?" he asked, feeling stiff and uncomfortable.

Gwyn looked at him, irritated. "I don't know," she snapped. "I'm not magic, you know."

"Oh, er, right, of course," said Gabe, embarrassed. He'd gotten so used to her having all the answers that he hadn't even thought about what a silly question that was.

Gwyn laughed at his expression. "Don't worry, Sandals," she said. "You'll be back in your robes before you know it. In the meantime, have a nap – and try not to snore louder than they do."

With that, Gwyn closed her eyes and promptly fell asleep, still sitting upright, as Gabe looked on in amazement.

Ouch! Gabe sat up, wincing at the thorns he could feel under his breeches. He rubbed his forehead groggily, wondering if he'd been stung as he slept. Something had certainly woken him up.

Ping! Another sharp pain, this time at the back of his neck. He looked around wildly – was he under attack? – and noticed that Gwyn had gone, leaving only a slight hollow in the brambles beside him. Even as he looked, a tiny rock smacked him on the end of his nose. Inhaling sharply, he looked up to see a pair of sparkling eyes peering at him through the thicket.

"Wakey, wakey," came Merry's taunting whisper, and Gabe heard subdued sniggers around her.

"Merry!" he said, relieved to see her, despite the rocks.

"Shh," she said, creeping through the brambles to sit beside him, and he realized that Dan and Hal were no longer snoring.

"What's going on?" Gabe asked, his mind feeling foggy. "Where's Gwyn?"

Merry didn't respond, simply parting the brambles in front of them so that Gabe could see through to the clearing. Dan and Hal were sitting up, facing them, and Gabe ducked instinctively.

"They can't see us," said Merry. "Look over there."

Lifting his head, Gabe followed her pointing finger and watched, mouth dry, as Gwyn stepped into the far side of the clearing, wearing one of the white masks that the girls reserved for holdups.

"What's she doing?" he hissed. "Is she mad?"

Merry laughed softly. "I think she probably is a little bit – but I'd call it angry rather than mad."

As she spoke, Gwyn slid two fingers up under the mask and whistled, a sharp, shrill sound that carried clearly across the clearing – and probably into the next shire, Gabe thought.

The two men leapt to their feet, turning towards the sound.

"Clear off, you ugly oafs!" Gwyn shouted. "You've no business here!"

Dan and Hal looked at each other, bemused, before bursting out laughing. "We do now," said Dan. "Ronan is going to love us for finding you, Tom Thumb. Small question of a missing horse . . ."

"Oh ho," said Merry, clearly enjoying herself. "She's going to love being called Tom Thumb."

Gwyn responded by walking to the oak tree and reaching up into a low branch, pulling down a crossbow she'd hidden in the leaves. In one swift motion, she raised it to her shoulder and drew back the string, sending a bolt hurtling across the clearing at the two soldiers, who jumped as it landed in the dirt in front of them.

"I won't miss with the next one," she told Dan and Hal, already laying the next bolt as the soldiers looked at each other, eyebrows raised. In response, they pounded across the clearing towards her, screaming abuse. Gwyn merely turned and ran lightly into the thicket opposite.

"Aren't you worried they'll hurt her?" asked Gabe, taken aback at Gwyn's actions. Dan and Hal didn't hesitate at the thorny thicket, charging into the brambles, following the path Gwyn had taken.

Merry looked at him sideways. "They'll have to catch her first."

As the soldiers disappeared into the woods, making as much noise as a pair of wounded bulls, Scarlett, Midge and Eddie crept up beside Gabe and Merry.

"How long will it take her to lose them?" Scarlett asked.

"She said she's going to take them round and round in circles," said Merry. "Less chance of them remembering how to get back here that way. She'll be a while."

Gabe stretched, feeling his arms and legs protest at the movement. He wondered just how long he'd been asleep. Looking up, he could see that the sun was sliding down towards the tops of the trees and the moon was on the rise. Despite his nap, it had been a long day.

"Where have you been?" Gabe asked Merry, through a yawn. "We waited and waited . . ." He stopped.

"Did Gwyn tell you what we saw?" Gabe asked, suddenly alert. "Did she ask about *him*?"

He nodded at Eddie, who had said nothing and was looking very pale and miserable.

"She did," said Merry, "and we'll talk about it soon. It was more important to get rid of those dolts first. But he does have a lot of explaining to do. About why he put us all in danger by refusing to go to the Abbey, for one."

Eddie, red-faced and narrow eyed, opened his mouth to speak, but closed it at a glare from Merry.

"We spent so much time arguing about it that the blasted soldiers nearly caught us," Merry went on, turning to Gabe. "It was only Midge hearing the horses that saved us."

Midge smiled modestly.

"Then the woods were crawling with men," Merry went on, shaking her head. "Everywhere I turned there was a soldier – even your lot were out, Gabe. A whole bunch of sandal wearers wandering about looking like they wished they were safely back behind walls."

Gabe frowned. That must have been Prior Dismas and the others, following the orders of the man in black.

"And they nearly caught us!" Scarlett was saying, indignantly. "It was only the villagers over the way hiding us that kept us out of the castle dungeon." Her face and hair were even dirtier than they had been that morning.

Merry smiled. "What goes around, comes around," she said to Scarlett, although she winked at Gabe. "We've helped them, they help us."

"Yes, well, I'd like to know just why so many men are so utterly keen to catch up with him," said Scarlett, pointing to Eddie.

"Me too," said Merry, standing up and dusting off her breeches. "And now seems as good a time as any to get the full story."

With that, she pushed her way out of the thicket and strolled across the clearing, leaving the others no choice but to follow. Gabe struggled to his feet, hoping that the full story might come with food attached. It had been a long and tiring day since breakfast and he was hungry.

"All right, Eddie," Merry said, mouth full of cornbread and dripping. "You're not the boy from the mill, though you look a lot like him. Who are you?"

Gabe put his own bread down, feeling his tummy swell. He'd been so happy when Merry had announced they'd eat, then talk, that he'd stuffed himself on Midge's excellent cornbread. Now he felt slightly ill.

"I," said Eddie, standing up, "I am Prince Edward, Crown Prince of Alban."

There was a short silence and then Merry and Scarlett burst out laughing. Gabe looked at Midge, who raised her brows back at him, seemingly as confused as he was.

"Good one!" shouted Merry, waving her cornbread at him. "Course you are!"

Eddie looked bewildered. "Why do you laugh?" he asked.

Scarlett wiped her eyes, still giggling. "Prince Edward of Alban? I don't think so," she said. "Who are you really?"

He sat down again, face serious. "That's who I am," he repeated. "I was on my way to Rothwell on behalf of my father, King Warwick, who has some . . . qualms about Lord Sherborne's accounting. My carriage was set upon by thieves and in the melee that followed, I was captured, bound and gagged."

Merry shook her head. "Don't be ridiculous," she said. "Thieves wouldn't have put you in the castle dungeon. Your story makes no sense."

Eddie looked close to tears. "I know," he said. "I don't know what happened. One minute I was fighting, the next I'd woken in the dark with a man – your father as it happens – who told me I was locked in a cell in Lord Sherborne's dungeon."

Scarlett looked perplexed. "But we'd know about it if the Crown Prince had gone missing," she said. "And surely you could have just asked to speak to Lord Sherborne?"

"I did!" said Eddie, smacking the floor in frustration. "I asked until I was blue in the face, explaining to that huge lunk of a guard that there'd been a mistake, but I was ignored."

Gabe and the girls all stared at him. "You don't act very princely," said Merry.

Eddie managed a tired smile. "How's a prince meant to act?" he asked.

"Hoity-toity," Merry responded, with fervor. "Rich, spoiled, arrogant . . . fake."

"Plus," Scarlett interjected, head cocked to one side, "no Prince would allow himself to be ordered about by Merry and Gwyn and you've been doing what you've been told from the start."

"I haven't had much choice," Eddie said. "Besides, my father always taught me that no man, not even the King, knows everything and when faced with superior knowledge, a great King uses it to his own end. I couldn't get out of there on my own, so I bowed to those who could help me do so."

But Scarlett was shaking her head. "No, no, no," she said. "You're not a Prince. You'd be spouting 'thees' and 'thous.' I went to court once with my father and couldn't follow the conversation half the time."

Now Eddie looked angry. "There hasn't exactly been an opportunity to show off my courtly manners!" he said.

Scarlett rolled her eyes. "Particularly when you don't have any," she said, dismissively. "You're not a Prince."

"I am, too!" he said, "And I can prove it."

"How exactly are you going to do that?" laughed Merry. "Show us how you sit on the throne? Make a proclamation? Take ten percent of our dinner away from us?"

Eddie frowned at the last, recognizing it as a jab at the hated tithing system, but he shook his head. "I've got the mark," he said.

Scarlett stilled. "You have not," she said.

"What's the mark?" asked Gabe.

"It's a tattoo given to royal babies," Scarlett explained. "All of them have it. It's in a secret location and only the King's closest advisors know what it is. It's so that imposters can't be substituted – babies tend to look very alike."

Gabe nodded, though in truth he'd never had much to do with babies.

"Well, I can tell you that it's a golden wolf tattooed between my toes," said Eddie, triumphantly, walking over to where Scarlett and Merry were sitting. "Look!"

He removed his boot and Gabe noticed for the first time that whilst he wore the coarse-woven tunic and hose of a farm laborer, his knee-high boots were made of some kind of soft leather, which was looking the worse for wear. Then Eddie slipped off his thin sock and thrust his foot into Scarlett's and Merry's surprised faces.

Scarlett wrinkled her nose as Eddie pried apart his big and second toes, but seconds later she gasped, hand over her mouth.

"He's definitely got a tattoo," she said. "It's tiny, it could be a dog, but it's there."

"It's not a dog!" Eddie said, snatching back his foot.

Merry got to her feet, pacing the room, ignoring both of them. "That's as may be," she said, picking up a teacup from the shelf and examining it closely, "but we've only his word for it that this particular tattoo is the secret mark. For all we know they tattoo their babies with a duck or a turnip."

Midge and Scarlett giggled and Merry winked at them before turning to Eddie, who looked as though he was about to explode. "I'm telling the truth!" he declared, sitting down to pull his sock back on. "My father and I both have the mark. It's our family crest."

Merry acted as though he hadn't spoken, turning the teacup over and over in her hands. "Did my pa believe your story?" she asked, after a long pause. "Is that why he insisted we take *you* with us – and not him?"

The pain on Merry's face told Gabe how much she had hated leaving her pa behind in that dungeon.

"He did," said Eddie, quietly, now pulling up his boot. "I'm sorry, Merry – I know how much it hurt you to leave him, but he was sick and . . ."

His words drifted away and Gabe could see that he knew that to go on would not make the situation better. *He knows how to read people*, Gabe thought. Brother Malachy, who'd always been given to airing his thoughts aloud on any subject, had once lectured Gabe about the importance of learning to understand that what people said and what they did were often two different things – and that what they did counted for more. Now Gabe watched Eddie closely, noticing how he stood with his hands clenched beside his body, appearing to steel himself against the harshness of Merry's gaze.

"Why?" she asked. "Why did he believe you?"

Gabe held his breath, knowing that this was perhaps the most important question so far. Merry held her father in such high esteem that if he believed Eddie, then she would, too.

"I told him the whole story," Eddie began, "and, frankly, his first response was very similar to yours."

"He laughed?" asked Merry.

"Well, he wasn't that rude," said Eddie, glaring at Scarlett, "but he certainly treated me as though I was addle headed."

Merry smiled. "And then?"

"We began talking about other things, just to while away the time," said Eddie. "I told him about my childhood and my father . . ."

"The King?" interjected Scarlett, and her disbelief was obvious.

"The King," repeated Eddie. "Eventually, he began to ask me questions and – I think I just had too many details for him to discount. But it wasn't until we started discussing *him* and the things that had happened to *him* and the things that he'd heard down in the dungeons that we began to put two and two together."

"He was wrongly arrested," said Merry, pacing. "He's not a poacher, he's a woodsman – the best that Lord Sherborne has ever had."

Eddie nodded, face sober. "He told me and I believed him," he said. "But he thinks – and I agree – that he saw something out there in the woods that he shouldn't have seen and that's why he's been punished."

"But what?" Merry asked, frustrated. "What could he possibly have seen?"

"I asked him and he said he's been over it and over it a thousand times in his mind and he doesn't know," said Eddie. "What he does know, though, from things he's heard, is that all is not well with Lord Sherborne. Your father says that Harald – you know, the mountainous guard? – is always complaining that his wages are late or short."

Merry appeared to mull this over. "So Lord Sherborne is short of gold, is he?" she mused, looking meaningfully at Gabe. "He'd be looking for it, then?"

Taken aback, it took Gabe a moment to put two and two together and come up with Prior Dismas, the velvet-cloaked men and the golden cover he'd returned to the Abbey. Had the Prior been acting on Lord Sherborne's instructions?

Gabe's hands clenched. The Abbey's treasures were not the property of one man. They were kept inside the walls to help safeguard them for generations to come. To think that the Lord would abuse his patronage like that!

"He is," Eddie was saying. "That's one reason I am here. Father sent me to find out why the tithe from this shire has been . . . lacking of late. Tales have reached the palace that people are starving here because Lord Sherborne takes everything – but he tells my father he has nothing. When your father heard that, he believed me."

Scarlett was shaking her head. "It still makes no sense," she said. "Gabe returned the gold cover, so there's the gold for Lord Sherborne – and there's absolutely no reason why keeping the Crown Prince in his dungeon would be of any benefit whatsoever for Lord Sherborne. If he intends to send a ransom note, the King would simply send his whole army down here to rescue his son."

Eddie nodded gloomily. "I know," he said. "I've racked my brains but I can't see the angle. If I could, I might be able to fight it."

"If you truly are the Prince," said Midge, shyly, "then surely you could simply march up to the castle and demand your soldiers arrest Lord Sherborne and anyone else you suspect might be in on the plot?"

Merry looked up. "And then you could release my pa!" she said, fiercely.

"I would," said Eddie, gravely. "I will."

Scarlett laughed harshly. "Now you sound as though you believe him," she said to Merry, jumping to her feet. "Surely you don't actually think this upstart is Prince Edward?"

Merry looked torn, and Gabe knew she wanted to believe Eddie more than anything, mostly because her father would be freed. But she hadn't survived in the woods for this long without being as wary as a forest animal.

"We need to know more," Merry decided eventually, tossing the teacup in the air and catching it neatly with one finger through the tiny handle. "You can stay with us for the time being, seeing as Pa asked us to take you. But if your story doesn't check out, we'll take you deep into the forest and leave you to the foxes."

"And when it does?" asked Eddie, standing with his hands on his hips, tall and defiant. Gabe wondered if it was just his imagination that the older boy suddenly looked bigger, stronger and – regal.

If Merry noticed it, she showed no sign. "*If* it does," she said, "we'll have some apologizing to do, won't we?"

Eddie nodded curtly. "And there'd better be a few 'thees' and 'thous' in it for good measure," he said, glaring at Scarlett, who smirked.

"All right," said Merry, "that's enough. Gabe, have you checked on your package?"

"I have," he said. He'd waited until Eddie had entered the oak before ducking around the back and climbing up into the canopy to reassure himself that the cipher, wrapped in oiled cloth to protect it from moisture, was still in the small hollow in which he'd left it. Albert stood sentinel nearby.

Now that Gabe was wearing breeches, his pocket wasn't big enough for the book, so he'd decided to leave it where it was for the time being. He'd hoped he would get some time later that night to examine it again, looking for a clue as to what it was and what he should do with it next.

But with Eddie's presence in the camp now, Gabe wondered when he might get that opportunity. He certainly didn't want to bring the book out in front of the other boy, and the way Merry was referring to it as a "package" gave him the message that she didn't want Eddie to know about it either.

"What do we do now?" he asked.

"Now," said Merry, "we wait for Gwyn."

"She'll be back any minute now," said Merry. He couldn't see her very well in the moonlight, but Gabe could hear the anxiety under the confident tone. All through the long night, they'd been waiting for Gwyn, jumping at every sound, but she hadn't appeared. Now they were all sitting outside in the clearing, in the cold dawn light of the rising sun, but there was still no sign of her.

"Should we look for her?" asked Midge for the umpteenth time, but Merry simply shook her head as she'd done every time before.

"She could be anywhere," Merry said, wearily. "If we stay here, she knows where to find us."

"It's been too long," said Scarlett, squinting in the brightening light. "Where could she possibly have gone?

It wouldn't have taken her this long to lose those soldiers." There was a pause before Scarlett dared to speak the words they were all thinking. "Do you think she's been caught?"

Merry scoffed. "Of course not," she said. "Something else has come up. You'll see, she'll be here soon."

But Gabe noticed that she'd brought her long bow outside with her and kept it close to hand. He yawned, listening to the skittering sounds of small creatures in the surrounding thicket. It had been a long night and Eddie, in particular, was almost asleep sitting upright. Gabe felt sorry for him, realizing that he'd probably slept very little during his time in the dungeons and had had no time to rest since his escape.

Watching the other boy's eyelids drooping, Gabe wondered if it might be a good time to sneak off and see if he could take the cipher inside to study it more closely. He was just about to ease himself up on his knees to see if he could crawl away without rousing Eddie, when a voice spoke behind them.

"I wasn't expecting a welcoming committee."

Everyone was on their feet instantly, and Merry threw her arms around Gwyn, who looked small and pale, though Gabe noticed a dark bruise blooming on her cheek.

"Where have you been?" Merry asked. "I've been worried sick."

Gwyn tried to laugh but it came out more as a splutter. "It was a bit more complicated than I thought," she said.

"I'll tell you in a moment. Right now I need a drink and something to eat."

Midge ran off to do as Gwyn bid, and Merry hugged her sister tighter. "I thought you'd been caught," she admitted, leading Gwyn inside the oak.

"I was," said Gwyn, and Merry gasped in shock, "but only because I wanted to be. It seemed the quickest way to get to the castle."

"Is that where you got that bruise?" asked Merry.

Gwyn nodded. "Dan and Hal weren't too happy with being led a long and merry chase," she said. "But I made sure I was in the village before I let them catch up with me – lots of people around to make sure they didn't punish me too much for it."

"But why?" asked Scarlett, her eyes wide. "Why would you do that?"

"I wanted to have another go at seeing Pa," Gwyn said. "The dungeons were supposed to be open all day, you know, as part of the festival. My plan was to give Dan and Hal the slip once they'd gotten me to the gates, nip to the dungeons and then get back here. I thought if I could just talk to Pa we could come up with a plan for next time."

"Next time?" asked Gabe.

"Next time we go to get him," Gwyn said, her tone implying that this was a given.

Midge came in and handed her a plate piled high with cornbread, and a mug of milk. There was a pause while Gwyn gulped down the milk and had several big bites of bread.

"So what happened?" prompted Scarlett, as Gwyn's chewing slowed.

"It all worked perfectly," Gwyn said, sipping her milk. "But the dungeons had closed because everyone was at the tournament."

Now it was Eddie's turn to gasp. "What do you mean? How can that be?"

Gwyn looked at him strangely. "What do you mean?" she parroted. "The Prince arrived this afternoon and the tournament was underway."

"What?" Eddie shouted, looking wildly around the room. "How can the Prince have arrived when I'm here?"

Gwyn laughed, looking to her sister for an explanation. "He's here?"

Merry looked sad. "He says he's the Crown Prince, kidnapped and held in the dungeons," she said, shaking her head. Gabe could almost hear the "poor fool" that Merry left unsaid.

"I AM!" a red-faced Eddie shouted, looking as though he would burst at any moment.

"Well, I'm sorry to say that I saw the Prince sitting in the Royal Box at the tournament," said Gwyn, chewing thoughtfully on a piece of bread as she stared at Eddie. Suddenly, she put her bread down, her eyes widening.

"What is it?" Merry asked. "What are you thinking?"

"He looks like him," Gwyn said, pointing at Eddie. "Like the Prince, I mean. Eddie looks like the Prince."

This startling revelation silenced everyone in the room.

"You mean," Eddie said, "that the boy in the Royal Box *looks like me. I* am the Prince."

Merry frowned, as she stared into Eddie's face. "What if he's right?" she said, slowly to Gwyn. "What if the boy from the mill does *look like him*, rather than the other way around? Wouldn't that explain why Eddie was kidnapped? Why he was put in a dungeon. He was kidnapped because he is the Prince – and Lord Sherborne has put an imposter in his place."

Merry paused, before surmising. "He wants to control the Prince. It's the only thing that makes sense."

"Don't be ridiculous," snapped Scarlett. "You don't actually believe this upstart, do you? What good would *controlling* an imposter do Lord Sherborne?"

"I don't know," said Merry, shaking her head.

"I do," said Eddie. "My father – and this is not common knowledge – has been unwell. He thinks I do not know, but I see the court beginning to jostle for position, looking to me for favors. Perhaps Lord Sherborne knows this and hopes to install a puppet on the throne, bringing himself into a position of great power."

Gabe gasped. If Lord Sherborne was the power behind the throne, what would that do for people who had helped him along the way? People like Prior Dismas.

Merry shook her head. "I don't know what to believe right now," she said to Scarlett. "None of this makes sense, but he does have a mark, Scarlett. How many people would even know about that?"

"Anyone of noble birth," Scarlett said, her tone ice-cold. "*Anyone*. To make that mark worth anything, we need to know if the wolf is what they actually use."

Gabe stepped forward, between the two cousins. "I had a thought about that," he said.

"Well," said Scarlett. "Speak up then!"

Instead, Gabe turned to Gwyn. "Can you take a note to Brother Malachy?" he asked. The time that Brother Malachy had spent as part of the King's personal detail was about to come in handy . . .

"I'll do better than that," she said, putting her plate aside and rubbing her eyes. "I'll take *you* to Brother Malachy. He's at Rothwell Castle with all your other Brothers. They were honored guests of Lord Sherborne at the tournament yesterday and have stayed for the jousting this morning."

Gabe frowned. "The Abbey is empty?"

"Looks that way," Gwyn confirmed. "Judging by the numbers of robes I saw at the tournament."

Gabe thought about all that he'd seen and heard in the past few days, a jumbled collection of thoughts and images swirling through his mind like the mosaic tiles on the floor of the Abbey's chapel. He saw Brother Benedict bleeding on the cold stone floor. He saw Prior Dismas's thin face and Damman's heavy fists. He saw Ronan, threatening him with the dungeon. He saw the man in black on his thrashing horse out in front of the Abbey. And he saw the cipher.

It wasn't the cover of the cipher that Lord Sherborne wanted, no matter how valuable its gold and jewels might be, he realized. It was the book. And now the Abbey was empty . . .

"It's about the book," he said, ignoring Merry's frown and Eddie's confused expression. "It's all about the book. Lord Sherborne wants that book." Gabe turned to Gwyn. "We have to go," he said. "Right now. Will you take me to Malachy? I think the Abbey is in danger."

"Hold on there, Sandals," said Merry, striding over to grab his arm. He tried to throw it off, but she tightened her grip and he winced under the strength of her hand. "If you're going, we're going," she said, indicating the group. "All of us. We're going to settle this question of Eddie once and for all – and rescue Pa if we can."

"Yes, Winterfest is approaching," Scarlett said, absentmindedly.

"Winterfest is eight weeks away," Merry said. "What are you talking about?"

Startled, Scarlett looked at Gabe, who gulped. In all that had happened that day, neither of them had told Merry and Gwyn about Winterfest – and the fact that it was the date of their pa's hanging.

When Scarlett shook her head, refusing to say anything, Gabe realized it was up to him to share the bad news. Taking a deep breath, he told the girls what the guard had said.

"Hanged?" said Gwyn, and for a moment Gabe saw the little girl behind her worldly exterior. "How can this be?"

"The King's stag," said Gabe. "They're saying he killed the King's stag."

Merry gasped. "He never would!" she said, taking her sister's hand. "He'd never ever touch that stag. He loved that animal, used to tell us it was the symbol of all the best of the world." She turned to Midge. "Have you seen it? It's white all over – you can't miss it."

Sadly, Midge shook her head. "Nay, I've never seen it," she said. "There are three or four young bucks running with the herd at the moment, but no white ones at all."

"Where is it then?" asked Merry, aghast. "What's happened to it? If we can't produce it, we'll never prove Pa's innocence."

"You don't need the stag," said Eddie, stepping forward. "You've got me. I'll pardon him. I know he's done nothing wrong. He's not that man."

There was a silence, whilst Merry stared at Eddie, seeming to see right through him. "Or," she said, and Gabe could see her almost physically drawing on all her strength, "we'll simply rescue him now. As we said we would."

"But he can't even walk!" Scarlett said. "Remember?"

"One way or another, he's leaving that dungeon today," said Merry.

"We're wasting time," said Gwyn, still not looking at anyone in the room as she walked to the door where she'd dropped her crossbow. Nobody said a word as they collected their own weapons and followed her out into the sunlight.

CHAPTER TEN

"Please tell me we're not all going through that tunnel again," said Eddie. Crouched behind a sturdy elm tree in the shadow of the walls of Rothwell, Gabe agreed with Eddie. The thought of sliding through that narrow tunnel entrance again was enough to give him the shudders. Their position gave them a clear view of the Rothwell gates, and the long lines of people snaking down the road towards them.

"You're not," said Gwyn. "Midge and I are."

Gabe breathed a sigh of relief, though this quickly turned to horror when he realized that if he wasn't going through the tunnel, he was going in the front gate.

"Sandals," said Gwyn, turning to Gabe. "You and Scarlett use your papers again."

"What about me?" asked Eddie, and Gabe saw the impatience of a boy not used to following orders.

"You're with me," said Merry.

"How are we getting in?"

Merry grinned at Eddie, and Gabe was pleased to see the flash of white teeth. It had been a grim journey to Rothwell, with all of them following Gwyn's winding path through the woods in silence, their mood completely at odds with the beautiful autumn morning in the forest. Occasionally, Gwyn and Merry would whisper together, heads bent as they walked, formulating a plan.

"We're going in the back entrance," Merry said now. "I hope those boots of yours are sturdy."

Gabe looked down at Eddie's feet, noticing that his soft leather boots were now ripped and torn.

"I was dressed for traveling and greeting when I was kidnapped," Eddie lamented, looking at them. "Not for tramping in the forest."

"So you say," said Scarlett. "Or you stole a nobleman's boots and that's why you really ended up in that dungeon . . . Where are your other fine clothes?"

"I don't know," said Eddie. "I woke up in the cell, wearing these rags."

"Hmmph," said Scarlett, turning her face from his in disdain.

"Come on," said Merry. "Rags or no, we're off."

"Where to?" asked Eddie, slipping out from behind his tree before ducking behind the hedgerow.

"The stables," Merry said, looking up and down the road before darting across and disappearing into the trees on the other side.

Startled, Eddie looked both ways before scarpering after her.

"Get as close to the tournament as you can," Gwyn told Gabe and Scarlett. "We've missed the jousting, but we'll be just in time for the melee, I think, which is good cover for us."

Gabe felt a thrill of excitement at the idea. He'd never seen a melee, but Brother Malachy had described one to him and he could imagine the spectacle that it must be when two teams of horsemen attacked each other.

Of course, it was all in fun, Brother Malachy had said, with a faraway gleam in his eye. The idea was to force the other team back or break their ranks. Sometimes knights would fight each other on horseback or on the ground and a particular highlight was if a knight was captured and then ransomed off to his own team.

For a moment, Gabe forgot all about the book, Ralf Hodges, Eddie's claim to the throne and all the other reasons that had brought them to Rothwell – he just wanted to get a glimpse of the melee!

"I'll meet you under the stand," Gwyn was saying, taking Midge's hand and leading her away in the direction of the river. "There's only one. To the left of the Royal Box. Go and join the line."

Sighing, Scarlett picked up the replacement basket she'd been given, this time full of pears, with the two knives tucked back under the fruit. "Come on," she said, wearily. "Let's go."

Feeling in his pocket for their papers, Gabe steeled himself to face the scrutiny of the guards once again. He could only hope that they wouldn't have to weather any jokes about their "marriage" again today.

"Where are they?" muttered Scarlett for the umpteenth time. Having stood out in the sun for what felt like hours, passed through the gate and found their way to the tournament field, she and Gabe were now hidden under the nobles' stand.

"They've got farther to go than we had," said Gabe. "They had to get to the tunnel, through the tunnel and then past Harald and the gatekeeper to get out of the dungeon."

Above him, he heard a clang and a roar and wished again that Scarlett had let him stop for a few moments to see the tournament. The Grand Melee had begun and it was as noisy and exciting as he'd imagined.

"But what about Merry and Eddie?" said Scarlett, going on quite as though nothing was happening around them. It seemed that girls were not as interested in knightly fighting as knights might fondly imagine.

"I don't know where the stables are," said Gabe, struggling to shout over the howling of the crowd above him, "but it stands to reason that they had to walk farther and then it wasn't a simple matter of showing papers and walking in, I'd think. They'll be here."

"I can't bear just sitting here," Scarlett wailed. "You realize that my father is likely to be sitting in the stand above our heads."

Gabe grimaced. He looked at her, huddled miserably in the corner, her face dirty, her still-brown hair wild with knots and tangles. "He won't recognize you," he said, certainly, comparing her appearance with the picture he'd seen the day before, golden haired and well bred. "You don't look like yourself at all."

Scarlett's bottom lip wobbled, and her eyes filled with tears. "I hate this, you know," she confessed. "Merry and Gwyn, they're at home with the dirt and fending for themselves, but me . . ."

"You could go home?" Gabe suggested. "Your family is obviously looking for you."

"Never!" Scarlett said, wiping her eyes. "Not while my father is willing to marry me off to a man old enough to be *his* father."

Gabe said nothing, at a loss for words, and for a while the only sound under the stand was Scarlett's quiet sobbing, barely discernible over the hum of the crowd in the stands above them, and the stomping of their feet.

"What of your mother?" Gabe said, eventually. "What does she think of your father's plan?"

"She doesn't get to think," came Scarlett's bitter reply, as she dashed the tears from her face with the back of her hand, leaving white tracks in the grime. "Her thoughts, like mine, don't count, for we are not men."

There was nothing more to say to that and Gabe concentrated on listening to the sounds around him, trying to work out, from the roars and sighs, what was going on.

Moments later, Gwyn and Midge slid in beside them, as though being chased by hounds.

"Are you okay?" Gabe asked, leaping to his feet, preparing for flight.

"They've moved Pa," Gwyn said, her gray eyes wild and stormy. "He's not there anymore."

"Did you check the other cells?" asked Scarlett.

Midge nodded. "Nothing," she said. "All of that row has been cleared. There's nothing down there but mice and lice."

"What do we do now?" asked Scarlett.

"Wait for Eddie," said Gwyn, grimly, "and hope he is who he says he is because I think he's Pa's last hope."

"Stop the melee in the name of the King."

Gabe watched openmouthed as Eddie strode confidently into the middle of the ring, waving his arms, head held high, swords and shields flying around him. Even though he still wore the peasant's tunic, he walked as though a velvet cape swished around his thighs. The effect was somewhat tempered by the strands of straw in his hair and the horse manure that covered his breeches and boots.

Eddie and Merry had almost been caught in the stables, escaping only by slithering under a fence. To say that Eddie had been unimpressed was an understatement, Gabe thought, suppressing a grin as he thought of the other boy's face when they'd finally met up with the others.

The grin quickly disappeared, however, as he thought of Merry's distraught reaction to the news that her father was no longer in his cell . . . She'd quickly dispatched them all to different points around the field, holding Eddie back to whisper in his ear before sending him on his way.

"Stop, I say!" Eddie repeated now, his voice ringing across the tournament field, full of authority, and Gabe wondered if Eddie was playing his part in one of Merry's plans, or whether he was doing this all on his own.

Either way, Eddie had certainly grabbed everyone's attention. All around him, knights dropped their weapons, while the horsemen riding the perimeter of the field reined in their mounts in confusion.

Gabe licked his lips as the crowds – both the common folk massed around him and the nobles in the stand opposite – began to boo. Gabe focused on the Royal Box, noticing to his dismay that Prior Dismas was in residence, seated behind Lord Sherborne with Ronan of Feldham beside him.

There was no sign of the Abbot, or any other Brothers in any part of the crowd, and Gabe could only think that Gwyn had been wrong in assuming that they'd all stayed on overnight. On the plus side, this meant that the Abbey wasn't empty, and therefore open for anyone to wander in.

On the downside, it also meant Gabe needed to get to the Abbey to see Brother Malachy.

Now, though, Ronan was on his feet, hand on his sword, as though preparing to defend the figure in front of him – Crown Prince Edward, looking regal in a deep purple tunic embossed with a gold wolf, the symbol of Alban's royal family.

Gabe stared from the Prince, whose expression had not changed, to Eddie, red-faced and frowning.

"What is the meaning of this?" demanded Lord Sherborne, staring down at Eddie as though he were something the Lord had found in his chamber pot. "How dare you interrupt the Grand Melee!"

"How dare you place an imposter in my clothing!" Eddie shouted. "I have every right to interrupt anything I please. I am Crown Prince Edward of Alban."

In the silence that followed, Gabe could hear nothing but the jingle of the horses' bridles, the clank of metal as the knights removed their face guards to better see Eddie, and the steady hum as the crowd whispered.

Then Lord Sherborne began laughing, a rich, fruity sound, and the rest of the crowd joined in.

The Lord let them titter and shriek and chortle for a few moments, while Eddie's face grew redder and redder, though his expression remained blank. Then Lord Sherborne held up his hands for silence, before beginning to clap slowly. "Very nice," he said to Eddie. "I presume you are with the traveling players, adding to our entertainment today? But the joke is over and you will leave the field immediately."

"It is no joke – as you well know – and I will not leave the field until you have admitted wrongdoing and been arrested." Eddie stood tall and strong, his hand on his hip as though it was habitual for him to reach for a sword.

Lord Sherborne scowled. "Wrongdoing?" he said, with a fake laugh. "What wrongdoing would that be? If anyone is in the wrong here, it's you." He swished his velvet robe before sitting heavily back on his golden chair.

"Enough, my lord," said Ronan, stepping out onto the stairs of the Royal Box, his flat face grim. "We have entertained this fool too long. I shall arrest him now."

"You will do no such thing," said Eddie, standing his ground. "Where is Douglas Whitmore? Surely the Prince's personal guard is not far from the Prince?"

Now the crowd buzzed again, at Eddie's use of the guard's name. Ronan and Lord Sherborne spoke in low voices, before Ronan signaled to the bottom of the stairs.

Gabe's heart sank as the man in black stamped heavily up the stairs, bowing to Lord Sherborne. The sight of this man, who Gabe knew had conspired with Prior Dismas, confirmed for Gabe that Eddie's claim was true, and that he was also in great danger.

Gabe scanned the tournament crowd but could see no sign of Merry. It seemed she had delivered Eddie to the field and then disappeared, along with Gwyn, Midge and Scarlett.

Gabe couldn't begin to imagine how Eddie must be feeling out there in the center, no friends in sight.

"What say you, Whitmore?" asked Eddie. "Am I or am I not Prince Edward?"

He smiled, as though fully expecting his head guard to back his claim – a smile that drained from his lips as Whitmore opened his.

"The Prince sits behind me in the box," the man said tonelessly, though a crafty smirk played at his lips. "You, I do not know."

The crowd buzzed again, and the knights around Eddie put their hands on their swords. The fake Prince said nothing, continuing to stare blankly at the field before him.

But Eddie was not to be so easily dissuaded from his course, and now Gabe could truly see his new friend's regal bearing.

"I see," said Eddie, in a tone that suggested he truly did, and one that made even the man in black wince a little. "And yet I can prove my claim. You know I can."

"Come now," said Lord Sherborne, in fake hearty tones, shifting on his tapestry cushion. "This has gone too far. Run along back to your farm now, and we'll get on with the melee."

"No," said Eddie, striding across the field through slack-mouthed knights. "I have the mark and I will prove it."

Those in the noble stand gasped at his words, turning to whisper heatedly to each other. Eddie ignored them, taking the steps to the Royal Box two at a time. Three soldiers moved quickly to stand at the entrance between him and Lord Sherborne's coterie.

"Look!" said Eddie, shimmying out of his boot and sock and presenting his naked foot to Lord Sherborne. Gabe couldn't help but think that the royal family should have placed their tattoos in a more dignified spot . . . but then, he supposed, the idea was to hide the mark.

Lord Sherborne barely glanced at the proffered foot and merely smiled, an evil baring of teeth. "Very pretty," he said, standing and turning to the still blank-faced youth beside him, signaling a servant forward.

"But you see," said Lord Sherborne, as the servant quickly removed the "Prince's" footwear, "so does the real Prince!"

The crowd erupted as Eddie swayed, lost for words, and Gabe knew that the fake Prince, who still had not moved, bore the same mark as Eddie. His heart in his mouth, Gabe watched in horror as his friend began to back down the stairs, shaking his head.

"Seize him!" said Lord Sherborne, malevolently. "We will hang him today, this pretender to the throne."

The crowd cheered loudly at the idea of a public hanging, pressing forward, and the horses on the field began to dance nervously at the movement.

A sudden shove in the back almost sent Gabe to his knees and he turned to see the girls behind him.

"We've got to get out of here!" said Scarlett. "There's going to be a brawl!"

"We can't go without Eddie," said Gabe. "They're going to hang him!"

"Not if I can help it, they're not," said Merry, and with that she was gone. Watching her red hair darting through the crowd, Gabe realized that her bow was no longer across her shoulders.

Moments later, a barrage of arrows rained down on the field, first from the thickest part of the crowd, then from farther away, thrusting the knights and horses even further into confusion. Gabe kept his eyes glued to Eddie, who was ducking and weaving across the field, managing to stay one step ahead of Lord Sherborne's soldiers. The knights who'd been competing in the melee tried to stop him, but they were hampered by their heavy armor and he was able to keep moving.

"Seize him!" Ronan shouted, hoarse with anger and frustration, waving his sword above his head.

"Gabe," said Midge, grabbing his hand, "we need to do something."

"What can we do?" he asked, feeling very small in the pressing crowd. "He won't be able to keep out of their way much longer – they're too close!"

Gabe looked about wildly, searching for an answer – and as he did so, his eyes rested on Prior Dismas, on his feet in the Royal Box, shouting incoherently. Gabe gulped, knowing what he needed to do but wondering if he could.

Even as Gabe watched, the soldiers drew closer to Eddie, and the crowd in front of him massed together, forming a solid wall against his escape. Gabe knew he had to act, and there was only one thing that would divert Lord Sherborne's attention right now. "We need to create a diversion," he said to Midge. "Run to Merry and to Gwyn. Tell them I'm going to see the Prior."

"No!" Midge shouted in alarm. "They'll catch you."

Gabe looked down at her and smiled, with a calm he did not feel. "Tell Gwyn I'm counting on her to come and get me, okay? Go and tell her now."

Midge nodded soberly before disappearing into the throng of people now pressing against the flimsy barricades. Half the crowd was booing and hissing Eddie, throwing apples and pears at him in disgust. But there were others, Gabe noted with interest, who were more intent on trying to distract the knights and soldiers giving chase, running interference between them and Eddie.

Taking a deep breath, Gabe clambered over the barricades and into the field of fighting, hoping that one of Merry's arrows wouldn't hit him by mistake. He sprinted across the field and stood, staring up at the Royal Box, realizing that the only way to attract attention in the confusion around him was to be still.

As he'd hoped, his lack of movement soon drew all eyes in the Royal Box towards him and it took Prior Dismas only a moment to recognize him, despite the fact that Gabe wasn't in his customary robe.

"YOU!" the Prior shrieked. "Guards! Lord Sherborne! Ronan!"

The Prior was on his feet, dancing with rage, his face an unnatural shade of crimson. Gabe waited as long as he dared before turning and running back towards the barricades. Behind him, he heard Prior Dismas shouting to Lord Sherborne.

"THAT's the boy!" he shrieked. "The thief!"

"Aha!" said Lord Sherborne, in triumph. "Seize him!"

Now the level of confusion on the field was doubled as soldiers and guards, knights and squires, stared around them in doubt, wondering which boy to focus on. But as a huge knight in dark-gray armor reached out one hand to grab his shoulder, Gabe was heartened to see Eddie scrambling over the barricade in the far corner, almost unnoticed by the onlookers, who were now focused on this new entertainment.

"Don't move," came the knight's gruff voice, distorted by his heavy helm. "If you want to live, don't move."

Gabe nodded, giving himself up to his fate – and putting himself in the hands of Gwyn.

"Come with me," said the gruff voice, and Gabe followed meekly as he was led to the Royal Box where the Prior awaited him, a gleeful smile on his face, Damman leering behind him. Of the imposter Prince there was no sign.

"Where is it?" the Prior demanded as Gabe was shoved to the ground at his feet.

"Where's what?" asked Gabe, trying to twist his face into a mildly quizzical expression, glad his breeches protected his knees from the rough timber floor.

"Don't play games," said Damman, looming into view. "You know what he's talking about."

But Gabe merely frowned, knowing that the longer this conversation went on, the longer Eddie had to put as much distance as possible between Lord Sherborne and himself.

"Enough!" roared Lord Sherborne. "If this fool of a boy has the book, as you say he does, then I want it and I want it now."

"Oh," said Gabe, playing dumb, trying to work out what to do next. "The book. I don't have it." Gabe took a deep breath. "The book is in the Abbey," he lied, hoping the burning he could feel on his face wasn't showing up too much. He hated lying. It went against everything he'd ever been taught, but he suspected he would do it again – and probably worse – to keep the book safe.

"The Abbey?" Prior Dismas was shaking his head. "It's not there. We've searched."

"I, er, hid it," said Gabe. "In my secret place."

Lord Sherborne let out an exasperated sigh. "What is he talking about, Dismas? You told me that you'd searched *everywhere* and the only place the book could be was with this boy."

"The boy is a foundling," Prior Dismas responded waspishly, pacing back and forth in front of Gabe. "He has been at the Abbey since he was a babe in arms. He's had a lot of time to discover secret nooks and crannies."

"Where is this secret place?" demanded Lord Sherborne, looming over Gabe, his breath hot on the top of Gabe's head. Gabe stared at the Lord's boots, which, he noted with interest, had pictures of the Lord's own face tooled into the leather.

Thinking fast, Gabe decided that if the Lord thought he was a fool, now might be a good time to reinforce that opinion. "Oh, I forget," Gabe said, wincing as Lord Sherborne raised his fancy boot to kick him.

"Sire," came Ronan's smooth voice from behind Gabe. "There is a crowd."

Lord Sherborne paused mid kick and scanned the growing circle of nobles gathering around them, before straightening up and smoothing his velvet tunic. Gabe sent up a small thank you to the heavens that Lord Sherborne's desire to save face in front of his peers was greater than his desire to kick him to kingdom come.

"Perhaps I could find out more for you?" Ronan asked, his question trailing away delicately. Gabe shuddered at the thought of being placed in the Sheriff's hands and disappearing into the dungeons.

"I'll show Prior Dismas," Gabe said. "No other."

"You'll do as you're told!" Lord Sherborne blustered, but Gabe could see Prior Dismas preening and the look of cunning that crossed his face.

By placing the book in Prior Dismas's hands, Gabe knew he was offering the man power, and he hoped that it would be enough for the Prior to do as Gabe wanted – get Gabe into the Abbey where he could see Brother Malachy and where Gwyn had (hopefully) a better chance of getting him out than she would if he were buried in the castle dungeons.

"No," said Prior Dismas, rubbing his hands together as he walked towards Gabe. "The boy knows me. He will show me." He dragged Gabe to his feet, putting one arm around him. "Or else," he said, pinching Gabe hard under his armpit.

Wincing again, Gabe managed a smile. "Of course," he said, between clenched teeth. "Prior Dismas is my protector, after all."

As the Prior led him away from the tournament field, towards the main gates, with Damman and his other henchmen looming silently behind, Gabe's eyes searched the jeering crowd for a glimpse of the girls, but saw nothing.

He could only hope that Midge had passed on the message and that, even now, they were making their way to Oldham Abbey.

It was funny, Gabe thought, stumbling over a cobblestone, how incredibly alone a person could feel, even when surrounded by hundreds of people.

Gabe knew his hand was in front of his face because he could feel it. He could not, however, see it. He felt his way around the walls, cringing at the cold slime on his fingertips before carefully pacing out the confines of his cell. Four paces across, six paces long.

Gabe shuddered, thinking that if he'd been just a little taller, he wouldn't even be able to lie down in this terrible place. Not that he had any plans to do so just yet, given the damp rising up, even through his boots.

"Boo!" he said out loud, just to hear a voice. The sound seemed to be sucked up by the darkness, coming out as little more than a whisper. Gabe wondered just how far underground he was – and if anyone, let alone Gwyn, would ever find him again.

"Boo yourself," came a tiny voice in the dark, and Gabe jumped. He was in this dungeon alone. Who was talking to him?

"Hello?" he said, hoarsely. "Who's there?"

"Gabriel," came the voice, and now Gabe recognized it as a tired, faint echo of the Abbot's gentle tones.

"Abbot Phillip?" Gabe asked in wonder, walking towards the wall and feeling along it. Was it his imagination or did this surface feel rougher, less uniform than the others? "Is that you?"

"Indeed," said the Abbot.

"Are you all right?" asked Gabe. It was difficult in the dark to tell exactly where the Abbot's voice was coming from, but he certainly wasn't inside the cell with Gabe, so he could only assume he was on the other side of the wall. Gabe wondered how he'd lived his whole life in the Abbey and never known about these secret cellars, deep below the chapel floor.

There was a muffled chuckle. "All right might be stretching it," said the Abbot, and Gabe was alarmed at how faint his voice was. "But I still have a little water and . . ." The words drifted away, and Gabe gasped as he took in the implications of what the Abbot was saying.

Had he been down in a dark cellar since the night Benedict had given Gabe the book? Or even before? Remembering Brother Benedict's bloody gash, Gabe shuddered, hoping the Abbot hadn't been similarly mistreated.

"Have you food?" Gabe asked, urgently.

"No more," whispered the Abbot and Gabe's worst fears were realized. The Abbot had been left down here to die.

"Don't talk," Gabe said. "Save your strength for our rescue."

Again, there was a muffled laugh, but the Abbot said no more.

Even knowing that the old man was just on the other side of the wall, Gabe felt lost. He supposed he should be grateful – and Prior Dismas had told him as much – that he was back in the Abbey in this secret place, rather than in the castle dungeon under the care of Ronan of Feldham. But somehow, Gabe wasn't feeling particularly thankful.

It was a shame that his own "secret place" didn't exist.

Gabe sighed, touching his face and wincing at its puffy tenderness. He suspected his bruises were almost as dark as this cellar, a small reminder of what awaited him next time the trapdoor to the cellar opened.

Prior Dismas had not been happy to discover that Gabe would not immediately lead him to the "secret place" in which the cipher was supposedly hidden. Instead, Gabe had feigned forgetfulness, taking the Prior and his team down to the Abbey's kitchen garden, with its plots laid out in neat rectangles, each divided by a narrow, cobbled path. Low stone walls surrounded each bed, and it was to the longest of these that Gabe pointed.

"It's over there," he said, "behind the largest stone."

"You put the Ateban Cipher behind a rock in the garden!" Prior Dismas exploded. "It could have been damaged!"

Tucking away the name of the book in the back of his mind, Gabe wondered how Prior Dismas would feel if he knew that the cipher was really hidden in a hollow in an oak tree.

"Oh no," Gabe said. "It fit very well between the stones."

"Which one?" asked Damman, impatiently, looking at the hundreds of stones that had been carefully fitted together to create the drystone wall.

"Hmm," said Gabe, pretending to consider. "I think it was this one." He walked over to a large stone in the very center of the wall.

"Pull it out then! We haven't got all day," said Prior Dismas.

Gabe fitted his fingers around the stone, marveling at how smooth its edges were. The garden had been here for as long as he could remember, and much longer than that, the stones in the wall now almost polished by their time in the elements.

"Oh," he said, trying to sound surprised, "it's not moving. It mustn't be this one."

The Prior and Damman looked at each other. "Which one is it then, you stupid boy?" asked Prior Dismas.

"It must be this one," said Gabe, moving to the next stone. But, of course, it wasn't. As far as Gabe knew, none of the stones in the wall moved – but he figured they could spend a lot of time here, trying to make it happen.

Now, standing in the cold, dark cellar, Gabe thought wistfully of the hour or so he'd spent in the hot sun trying to find his secret place, with the Prior growing evermore restless and frustrated with Gabe's efforts.

Bees buzzed through the calendula, planted around the edges to attract them in to the garden bed, and he could smell the rich earthy scent of soil that had been recently fertilized with cow dung. It was this aroma, he suspected, that kept the Prior standing well back from the wall, a fact for which Gabe was grateful as he suspected it stopped him from getting an occasional clip around the ear.

Now Gabe wondered how long the Prior intended to keep him down here in the dark. He'd been shoved in through the trapdoor by Damman, landing with a thump on the damp floor, smashing his face into the stones.

"This had better help your powers of recall," Damman had threatened, standing over the trapdoor, looking down at Gabe, blocking the light. "We'll be back in the morning and you'd best have remembered by then or it'll be curtains for you. Ronan is waiting."

Now Gabe reached up overhead to feel the outline of the trapdoor for the umpteenth time. It was solid and fitted so that there wasn't so much as a crack of light filtering through. He could feel the thin indentation where the door and the wall met, but that was all. It was even too small for him to wedge his fingers inside.

Gabe had also tried pushing the trapdoor upward with all his might. But his efforts made no discernible impact on the wood, and he'd resorted to pummeling it with his fists, shouting and screaming, hoping to attract attention from a curious Brother.

Nothing.

It seemed he was going to have plenty of time to atone for his little white lie to Prior Dismas.

Gabe crouched in a corner of the cellar, wrapping his arms around his knees and trying to keep the seat of his breeches off the floor. He couldn't fathom how he was going to get himself out of this mess – and the Abbot. There didn't seem to be any way out, and he couldn't imagine how Gwyn would even find him, let alone help him escape, despite his positive words to Abbot Phillip.

The fact was that he didn't have the cipher to give Prior Dismas, and there was no way he could tell him where it was without giving away the girls' hideout. What would happen to it now? Would the girls use it to get their pa out of the dungeon?

Gabe sighed, close to tears, aware that he had let down Brother Benedict, unable to carry out what were probably his last wishes. He hadn't even found out who Aidan was, let alone taken the Ateban Cipher to him. And now he was letting down the Abbot, silent in the cell beside him.

All Gabe could hope was that Prince Edward had gotten away and was safe, for it seemed a shame to have given his life for nothing.

CHAPTER ELEVEN

A scuffling sound woke Gabe from a fitful sleep. He sat up slowly, feeling his knees and elbows protesting as he stretched out his arms and legs. He had no idea how long he'd been curled up in the corner; no idea how many hours had passed since he'd been thrown into this damp place.

Rubbing his eyes, he listened hard, hoping the scuffling wasn't a large rat, come to nibble on his toes.

Again, there was a faint rustling sound and Gabe cocked his head, trying to work out which direction it was coming from. It was hard to get his bearings in the solid dark – if it wasn't for the fact that the floor was beneath him, he'd have had trouble working out which way was up.

Suddenly, the trapdoor above him opened and a lantern was dangled down into the hole, blinding Gabe, who tried to disappear into the corner, his arms over his eyes. He didn't even look up, not wanting to see Damman's smug, malicious face.

"There's nowhere to hide, you know, Sandals," came a conversational voice from above.

Staring up into the lantern in disbelief, Gabe shook his head. It couldn't be.

"Well, are you going to sit there all night?" asked Gwyn. "Mal and I are fairly exposed up here."

Mal? Surely she couldn't mean . . . ?

"Gabe, are you all right?" came Brother Malachy's anxious voice. "We came as soon as we could . . ."

"You lot have far too many events in this chapel," said Gwyn, continuing to chat as though they were sitting outside the oak tree. "And Mal here tells me they'll all be trooping back in here in less than an hour, so the time to move is now."

Gabe got to his feet on shaky legs. "How did you ever find me?" he asked in amazement.

"Midge said you were expecting me," was all Gwyn said. "We can discuss the how of it later, once we've left this place far behind."

"Come," said Malachy, and Gabe could now hear the nerves under the man's gruff tone. "We have to leave now, Gabe. Nicholas is waiting."

Nicholas?

"I'll need your help to get out," said Gabe, stretching up his arms and feeling Brother Malachy's hands grasp his to pull him upward. Soon he was lying, gasping, on the cool mosaics, bathed in the glow of candlelight, staring up three tiled steps to the pulpit, which rose at the front of the chapel. On the other side of the pulpit were the rows of simple pews in which the Brothers sat six times a day for thought and reflection.

How strange to think of them all sitting there while he was alone in the dark beneath their feet.

"Come," said Brother Malachy once again, "we must go."

"Wait," Gabe said. "The Abbot, he's down there somewhere. He was next to me."

Malachy's eyebrows flew up. "There's another cellar?" he whispered. "It was only through luck that we found the entrance to this one – I'd noticed unusual movement in and out of the chapel and remembered Brother Benedict once telling me about an anchorite's stronghold deep beneath the altar. He said it had only been used once by a monk whom most had considered quite mad."

"If he wasn't before he went in, he would have been soon after," said Gabe, shuddering. Anchorites were sometimes known as living saints; men who locked themselves away from this world to prepare for the next. But they usually chose larger strongholds with at least one window.

"I think the anchorite's space has since been made into two," said Gabe, thoughtfully. "The Abbot is in the other half and the wall between is rough."

He stopped, realizing what he was saying.

"They walled him in?" said Brother Malachy, eyebrows nearly reaching his gray hairline. "Dismas is more desperate than I thought. We must get the Abbot out!"

"We don't have time to dig him out now," said Gwyn. "We have to go!"

Brother Malachy frowned but nodded. "I will get him out as soon as I can," he said. "Although, I cannot hide him here and it is clear that he must be hidden."

Gwyn paused. "Take him to Goodwife Alice, in the hamlet near Featherstone," she said. "Tell her Merry asks that she hide him and take care of him until she returns. Tell the Abbot that once he gets stronger he's to help take care of Alice and her bairns until we get back."

Malachy nodded and asked no further questions.

"Come on, Sandals," said Gwyn, looking pleased with her plan and pulling him to his feet. "You did a good thing helping Eddie, even if you made a mess of it."

Strangely happy with this faint praise, Gabe allowed himself to be helped up.

"Here!" she said, passing him a bundle. "You'll be needing this."

To his surprise, it was his robes. "Where did you get these?"

"The oak, of course," she said. "I went there as soon as Midge told me what had happened. I figured the best way to get you out was if you looked like you blended in."

Gabe shook his head. She really did think of everything and she had covered a lot of territory to get there and back.

"Where are the others?" he asked, slipping the robe over his head, not bothering to remove the breeches and tunic underneath.

"Down in the stables," she said, shifting her crossbow to a more comfortable position on her back. "Eddie insisted on coming – something to do with you being a hero and saving him or some such. Hard to argue with a Crown Prince, even if he doesn't have a throne at this particular time."

Gabe smiled. "And Merry?"

"Well, once Eddie was coming, she had to come with her bows and arrows to protect him and once she was coming, well, Scarlett wouldn't stay behind, and then we could hardly leave Midge on her own, could we?" Gwyn's exasperation with having to travel with so many others was clear.

"Thank you," he said, and she laughed.

"Don't thank me yet," Gwyn said. "You might be out of the hole but we're not safe in the woods yet."

With that, she turned and crossed to Brother Malachy, who was standing anxiously by the door that led to the ambulatory, a covered walkway linking the altar to the smaller chapels on the east side of the church.

"Come, Gabe," said Brother Malachy, already disappearing into the passage, his robes flowing behind him. "We haven't much time."

❖

The stables were dark and silent and Gabe could see no sign of movement. Flattened against the stone wall of the blacksmith's workshop, he had a clear view of the low building that housed the horses, even though the moon was weak.

"Where are the others?" he whispered.

"Here," said Gwyn.

Behind the stable's wide timber doors, a horse whickered softly and Gabe heard the stamp of hooves on timber. That would be Borlan, who, as the Abbey's most valuable stallion, was kept in the best stable. All the other horses made do with floors of hard-packed earth and straw.

"What do we do now?" Gabe asked.

"Nicholas is waiting inside for you," said Brother Malachy in low undertones. Gabe nodded – that explained why Borlan was whickering instead of neighing loudly, kicking at his box and waking the world. The horse had a reputation for being ill-tempered and lashing out at anyone he did not know – or like.

Nicholas had always laughed about the fact that Prior Dismas kept a wary distance from the huge black horse, preferring to have a stolid old mare like Winnie saddled and waiting for him in the stable yards on the rare occasion he went riding.

"He has three horses saddled and will open the back gate as soon as you're ready. You must be prepared to ride hard and straight – the noise you make as you leave will be noticed."

Gabe nodded.

"You cannot return," Malachy said. "And this time I mean it. You haven't gotten away with this yet – and you will definitely not get away with it again."

Gabe said nothing.

"You still have the book?" Malachy asked.

"It's safe," said Gabe.

"Very well," said Malachy. "Retrieve it and then leave the forest, Gabe. Find Aidan. Do what Brother Benedict asked of you."

Gabe was struck by a sudden thought, remembering why it was that he'd wanted to see Malachy all those hours before at the tournament. "The mark!" he said. "Do you know what they use to mark the Crown Prince?"

He already knew the answer, deep in his heart, but he wanted it confirmed, wanted to know that he'd done the right thing.

Malachy frowned. "Why do you need to know that?" he asked.

"Tell me," Gabe pleaded.

"A wolf," said Malachy, looking left and right as though worried he'd be overheard. "A tiny gold wolf."

Gabe exhaled and even Gwyn looked relieved.

"Right then," she said. "Best we get both you and Prince Charming out of here then. Thanks for your help, Mal, and good luck with the Abbot."

She reached out and shook his hand.

"It's been . . . interesting," Malachy said, a bemused expression on his face. Gabe wondered if everyone looked like that the first time they met Gwyn. He suspected he still did.

"Go, Gabe!" Brother Malachy's anxious whisper broke into his thoughts and Gabe realized with a start that Gwyn was already disappearing through the stable doors on the other side of the courtyard.

He held out his own hand to say goodbye, but to his surprise the Brother pulled him into a fierce hug. "Stay safe," Malachy said. "And if I don't see you again, long life."

Fighting back tears, Gabe hugged the Brother back, realizing that this truly could be the last time he would be within the walls of this Abbey. Deep in his heart, he resolved to do all that he could to get back here, back to his home, back to the Brothers who were his only family.

"Go!" Malachy said, releasing him and giving him a little shove.

"Be careful," Gabe said, knowing that the Brother had taken a huge risk in helping them, and that he would take even bigger risks in saving the Abbot.

Malachy smiled. "Don't worry," he said. "I'll be back in my chamber before they even realize you're gone and I will make sure the Abbot is safe."

With that, he was gone, disappearing into the shadows.

Shivering in his damp clothes in spite of the warm night, Gabe scanned the courtyard for movement before running on his tiptoes across the cobbles towards the faint light that now showed under the stable door.

Inside, he found Nicholas checking the girth strap on a small gray horse.

"Ah, there you are," said Nicholas, as calm as if he'd simply been waiting for Gabe to get dressed for lauds. "That's everyone then."

"Thank you for this," said Gabe, fervently. "I hope you don't get into trouble."

"To be honest," said Nicholas, with a big, mischievous grin, "I hope I do. I'm hoping Prior Dismas will decide I'm not Brother material and send me home. I'm not cut out for this, but my ma has her heart set on it. I couldn't figure out how to get out of it without breaking her heart."

Gabe laughed. "And your pa?" he asked.

"Pa never wanted me to come here in the first place," said Nicholas. "He'll be happy to have me back on the farm." Gabe knew that Nicholas's family were freehold farmers, based near a village called Havenmill, though he wasn't sure where that was.

Before Gabe could ask, Merry and Scarlett emerged from another box, leading a saddled chestnut mare.

"Where are the others?" asked Gabe.

"Here," said Eddie, appearing from the largest box with Midge in tow. "He really is a beauty," he said to Nicholas. "But I wouldn't want to have gone in there without Midge."

"No," said Nicholas, looking at the small girl with obvious admiration. "I've never seen him respond to anyone like that, not even to me." He turned back to Eddie. "Are you sure you can handle him?"

"Yes," Eddie said confidently. "Midge and I will manage him between us."

"You're giving us Borlan?" Gabe asked in wonder. "The Prior will be furious!"

Again, Nicholas gave that mischievous smile. "I know," he said. "If losing the Abbey's most valuable horse to a bunch of thieves doesn't get me out of here, nothing will. Besides, Borlan deserves better than he gets here. No one rides him because they're all too afraid, and that just makes him wilder."

"I'm not afraid," said Midge.

"Nor I," said Eddie.

I am, thought Gabe.

"Okay, enough chat," said Gwyn, sliding in through the side door to the stables. "I've slipped the bolt on the stable entrance gates and opened one side – we'll need to move quickly now, because they won't miss the hooves on the cobblestones, no matter how quiet we try to be."

Nicholas gave the gray horse one last pat, resting his head near her ear and whispering something. "Okay," he said, standing upright. "The horses are all ready – you'll have to double, but they'll easily carry you."

"Gabe, you ride with Gwyn . . ." Merry said, before pausing. "You *can* ride, can't you?"

Gabe looked at his feet. "A little," he admitted. All the foundlings and oblates had taken basic riding lessons when they were children, but it was only those who elected to work further in the stables who got really good at it. Gabe's six months of lessons suddenly felt like a very long time ago.

"Come on, Sandals," said Gwyn, already mounted on the gray. "Jump up behind and let's go. Oh, and take that robe off."

Realizing how difficult it would be to sit astride in his robe, Gabe quickly slipped it over his head and stuffed it down the front of his tunic.

"Why not leave it?" asked Gwyn.

"I might need it again," was all Gabe said, unwilling to explain to this cynical girl that he wanted to take part of the Abbey with him.

Nicholas clasped his hands and Gabe put his foot in the resulting loop and heaved himself up behind Gwyn. To his surprise, there was ample room for him, despite the lightweight saddle that Nicholas had fitted.

"What's her name?" Gwyn asked Nicholas.

"That's Bess," he said, giving her a final pat. "And the chestnut is Jasper."

Around him, the others settled on their mounts, with Merry taking Jasper's reins and, to Gabe's surprise, Midge holding Borlan's reins lightly in her hands. She looked tiny atop the huge black horse, even with Eddie sitting behind her, but Borlan stood quietly, his ears forward as though listening to the conversation around him.

"You'd better let him lead," said Nicholas, walking over to stroke the stallion's long, proud nose. "He's not a follower."

Midge nodded, and patted Borlan's neck before gently pulling the left rein and touching her heels to his side. He walked placidly forward and out the stable door and Merry followed close behind, holding her reins more tightly to keep Jasper under control.

"Thank you, Nicholas," said Gabe, as Gwyn touched her heels to Bess's side and they began to move away. "Thanks for everything."

"Good luck!" Nicholas whispered, closing the stable doors behind them as they made their way as quietly as possible to the gate. Gabe noticed that it wasn't as dark outside as it had been, though the sky above was cloudy, and that a layer of dew seemed to have settled across the courtyard. It wouldn't be long now before the bells for matins would ring and the Abbey would be abuzz with movement. How long would it take the Prior to discover that Gabe was missing?

"Don't worry, Sandals," Gwyn murmured, without turning to look at him. "As soon as we're through the gates, we'll be away."

Taking a deep breath to try to relieve the unbearable tension that was ballooning through his body, Gabe counted out the steps to the gate. Twenty. Ten. He looked up as they passed under the stone arch as Bess plodded through the gate, leaning back so that he could see it longer.

Sitting upright, he could see the other two horses disappearing across the road and into the woods. To his surprise, Bess stopped walking.

"Get off and close the gate," said Gwyn. "Let's keep them guessing as long as possible."

Gabe slid from Bess's back and ran to the huge timber door, grabbing the ring and pulling as hard as he could. Through the rapidly narrowing opening, he caught a glimpse of the courtyard inside, just as the bells for matins began their slow, sonorous ring – Damman rounded the corner. Gabe gasped as the door slammed shut, a moment too late, for he had seen the expression on Damman's face and knew that the other boy had seen him.

Damman's shouts of alarm created a counterpoint to the ringing bells as Gabe ran back to where Bess was now stamping on the road, dust flying up around her hooves.

"Get on!" shouted Gwyn, reaching down to grab Gabe under the armpit to help haul him up onto Bess's back. He'd barely gained his seat before she dug her heels into Bess's side, forcing him to grab her around the waist and hold on tight.

Behind him, he could hear more shouts.

"Don't worry, Gabe," Gwyn shouted over her shoulder. "It'll take them time to get organized to chase and by then we'll be deep in the woods. Just keep your head down."

But Gabe couldn't help but look behind him, to see the Abbey gates creaking open and a crowd of brown-robed figures behind it, with Damman at the head. "There!" the boy shouted, pointing directly at Gabe. "It *is* him!"

As Bess picked up speed and hurtled towards the trees, Gabe's last view of his home of fourteen years was of an angry mob waving their fists at him. Taking Gwyn's advice at last, Gabe turned to face forward and kept his head down.

Gwyn rode Bess straight into the forest for half an hour or so before turning right and taking her into a shallow stream, which they followed for what felt like hours.

Just as the sun was rising, and Gabe thought he was going to fall asleep, she suddenly rode out of the stream, cutting through the forest again and out onto the road. Looking about him, Gabe could see that they were not far from a small village and Gwyn rode Bess right through the small settlement to a tumbledown farmhouse at the far end of town.

Here, Gwyn dismounted neatly, while Gabe nearly fell off the back of the poor horse, so stiff were his legs. She then led Bess and Gabe around the back of the farmhouse to a stone outbuilding set way back in the trees behind the house. All of this was done in silence. When she opened the outbuilding's ancient timber door, there inside, happily eating oats, were Borlan and Jasper.

"Right," said Gwyn, dusting off her hands once she'd tied Bess loosely to a post and given her some food. "Let's go. You can leave the robe for now – you won't need it."

Gabe reached into his tunic and pulled the robe out, tucking it into the corner of a stone shelf to keep it safe from inquisitive horses who might decide it was food. He stepped out of the building, pulling the door closed behind him, and started off towards the farmhouse, expecting that the others must be inside. It didn't take him long to realize that he was walking on his own.

Looking around, he saw that Gwyn hadn't moved and was standing by the trees, surveying him with an amused expression. "This way," she said, pointing into the forest.

"Where are we going?" he asked, jogging towards her.

"Home," Gwyn said, simply. "The others will meet us there."

The morning sun was hidden by gloomy, scudding clouds and Gabe was struggling to put one foot in front of the other as they trudged through the endless trees before they finally caught up with Merry, Scarlett, Midge and Eddie – all of whom looked much fresher than Gabe felt. He consoled himself with the thought that none of them had spent the previous night in a dark, stone hole.

"Not far now," said Merry, "and no sign of any other interested parties. We can lie low at the oak for a while and decide what we're going to do next."

Looking around him, Gabe wondered how she knew where they were. All the trees and clearings looked the same to him. Surely they'd passed that bluebell grove at least three times already that morning?

"What will happen to the horses?" he asked.

"They're safe for now," Merry said. "Farmer Hughes will look after them until we go back for them."

"How did you know you could take them there?" Gabe asked, beginning to wonder again about magic.

"We just know," said Merry. "Farmer Hughes knows us."

Meaning you've done him a favor at some point, Gabe thought, though he said nothing. He was beginning to realize that Scarlett's assessment of his worldliness was accurate and that he had no chance of surviving out here without Merry, Gwyn and the others.

Gabe wondered what Brother Malachy would do in the face of Merry and Gwyn's relaxed attitude to lying and crime, but rather thought that the older man would tell him to do whatever he needed to do to keep the book out of Prior Dismas's hands. Still, he found it troubling.

"Shh," said Midge, holding up a hand. All eyes turned to her as she stood, stock still, head cocked to one side.

"Something's wrong," she said. "Listen."

There was silence as they all did as they were told. "I don't hear anything," grumbled Eddie.

Midge smiled. "Exactly," she said, looking up at him. "No birdsong. Something's not right."

Gwyn frowned. "Maybe we've scared them off," she said. "Merry and Sandals were yabbering pretty loudly."

Gabe winced at "yabbering," but Merry poked her sister. "We were not 'yabbering,'" she said. "More likely they sense the growing storm!" She pointed up in the nearest oak tree, and Gabe could see chaffinches huddled right near the top.

Midge sniffed the air. "I smell smoke," she whispered, looking terrified.

Gabe took a deep sniff, noticing the others did too, and there, faintly beneath the cool, watery scent of bluebells, the sharp tang of burgeoning rain, and the musty aroma of the earth, he could smell wood smoke.

"It's not close," said Eddie.

"It's close enough!" said Scarlett, looking in alarm at her cousins, who'd gone white. Without saying a word, the sisters began running, disappearing into the trees ahead.

"Come on!" said Scarlett, taking off after them with Midge at her heels.

"What is it?" shouted Eddie. "What's happening?"

"I think it's the oak," gasped Scarlett. "I think it's our home."

Puffing like a kitchen bellows, Gabe burrowed into the brambles around the clearing with his heart in his mouth and Eddie at his side. Thick gray smoke filled the air around him and he couldn't see the others anywhere, but he could hear loud male voices shouting to each other on the other side of the thicket. Somehow, someone had discovered the clearing – and set fire to the oak in which the girls made their home.

Peering through the brambles, Gabe's heart sank. The tree's canopy was well alight, and a group of soldiers were standing together, cheering. Standing at the front of the pack, fists above their heads in triumph, faces wild with excitement, stood Hal and Dan, the two soldiers Gwyn had humiliated when she'd escaped from their custody at the Rothwell gates.

"Where are the girls?" Eddie whispered. "They can't go out there, those soldiers will arrest them – or worse – in an instant. We need to leave here – there's nothing we can do."

"But that's their home!" Gabe protested. "Everything they own is in there."

"What could they possibly have that's worth dying for?" Eddie hissed.

Gabe thought of their ma's precious crockery. "You wouldn't understand," he told the boy who, until this point in his life, had probably eaten from a gold plate every day.

Suddenly, Gabe stiffened in horror. He'd been so worried about the girls and their possessions that he'd almost forgotten his own precious item.

"Oh no!" he whispered, through lips suddenly frozen. "The book! The book is in that tree!"

Eddie stared at him. "The cipher? The one that Lord Sherborne wants so badly? You left it in a *tree?*"

"It was better than taking it with me and handing it over to them at the castle," said Gabe, stung. "I didn't have a lot of options."

"We're going to have to get it," said Eddie. "Without that book to bargain with, we have no chance of getting me back on the throne and the girls' father freed."

"It's not a bargaining tool," said Gabe, fiercely. "I have to take it to Aidan."

"You don't even know who Aidan is," said Eddie, his face set. "We will use the book as I see fit. I'm the Prince."

"We will not," said Gabe, hotly. "You are not currently a Prince – you're just a boy named Eddie – and I would rather let it burn than have it placed into Lord Sherborne's hands."

"You don't even know what it is!" Eddie said, red-faced with frustration. "Merry told me. She said you can't even understand what's written in it."

"I know that it's powerful enough for men to kill over it," said Gabe, stoutly. "Brother Benedict told me to take it to Aidan and that's what I intend to do."

"Yes, well, good luck with that!" shouted Eddie, using one hand to draw Gabe's attention back to the oak, which was now well alight. Gabe gulped, watching as sparks showered from the tree's canopy. The fire had not yet caught properly on the trunk, but it would be only moments before the entire tree went up in flames.

Gabe was struck by another horrific thought. "Albert!" he said. "Albert's tied up in the tree – right next to the book."

"Albert?" Eddie asked, but Gabe had no time for questions.

"I can't just lie here and watch Albert burn!" he said to Eddie, sliding forward on his stomach. "Midge will be devastated."

"What are you going to do?" hissed Eddie. "Are you mad?"

"I have to do something!" Gabe said, close to tears, reeling in horror for both the book and the magnificent bird. "I have to!"

He slid forward again, knowing that he would soon reach the edge of the thicket. The idea of having to face all of those soldiers and their weapons terrified him, but he could see no alternative. If he ran hard and fast into the fire, surely they wouldn't follow him. Then he could climb the tree and . . .

Just as he was realizing that his plan was not a plan at all, a hand clamped around his ankle and he was dragged backward through the thicket, crying out in pain as thorns caught on his face and ears.

"What in the name of all that is holy are you *doing*?" spat Merry. "Do you have a death wish?"

"The book," Gabe said, rolling over and sitting up to face her, his tears real now, though they were more about frustration than sadness. "I need to save the book. And Albert! Albert's in the tree!"

"And strolling across a clearing full of soldiers was going to save both of them?" Merry asked, as Midge and Scarlett watched on, their faces white, eyes big and solemn.

"I . . ." Gabe couldn't even finish the sentence. There was nothing to say.

Eddie reached over and patted him on the shoulder. "You did all you could," he said. "I'm sorry I said what I did."

Gabe nodded, keeping his eyes on the ground. "I'm sorry too," he said. "And girls, I'm so very sorry about your home, about Albert, about . . . everything."

When Merry didn't speak, he looked up at her, to find her staring across the clearing, her eyes full of tears. He looked around.

"Where's Gwyn?" he asked, slowly, suddenly feeling scared. "*Where is she?*"

"She's gone where she wants," said Merry. "Like she always does."

Hardly daring to look, Gabe turned back towards the clearing. The soldiers had stopped cheering and were standing in horrified silence as a tiny figure, wrapped from head to toe in cloth, disappeared into the flames, swinging itself into the only section of branches that was not yet alight.

Long seconds passed, and then a furious shrieking could be heard over the roar of the fire, and Albert suddenly erupted through the leaves, careening upward like an arrow shot from a bow towards the gloomy clouds.

The soldiers in the clearing followed his path to the sky with their eyes, missing the moment that Gwyn reappeared briefly to open the door to the oak. Gabe could hear the roar of the fire, popping and crackling as it gained momentum.

"*What is she doing?*" Gabe whispered in horror.

"Ma's crockery," Merry said. "She won't go without it. It's all we have left of her."

Now the soldiers were shouting and yelling, with one or two of them braving the heat from the fire to run towards the tree.

"Midge! She needs help," said Merry.

Midge nodded, putting her fingers between her lips and producing a long, shrieking whistle that stopped Albert mid flight. At a second whistle, he suddenly swooped towards the soldiers, who threw themselves to the ground trying to avoid his wicked yellow talons.

Despite the flames eagerly licking their way up the tree, hot and high, Gabe couldn't take his eye off the majestic bird as Albert again swept upward before hurtling back down towards the solders, diving again and again.

"Time to move them on so Gwyn can get out," said Merry after a minute or two, trying to sound confident.

"She won't get out!" Eddie said. "You should have stopped her!"

Merry shook her head. "You don't know Gwyn," was all she said, reaching for her bow and nocking an arrow. She nodded to Midge, who whistled again – three short piercing pips.

At her signal, Albert pulled out of a dive and began to lazily circle the clearing, keeping well away from the burning tree.

Merry stood suddenly and Gabe watched in amazement as she loosed arrow after arrow in quick succession into the group of hapless soldiers in the clearing.

Dan was shouting at them, trying to rally them, drawing his weapon and looking left and right for the source of the arrows, but the other men had had enough. The small figure striding into the huge fire had spooked them, the great bird swooping them had terrified them, and now arrows raining from nowhere set them to flight. Dan and Hal hurled abuse after their friends, but as the last soldier left the clearing, they looked at each other and then hurtled after him.

Even as they did so, the door of the oak opened again and Gwyn stumbled out.

"Come on!" said Merry, dropping her bow and shoving through the thicket towards her sister. Gabe and the others ran after her, and they met the coughing, spluttering Gwyn just as she stumbled, taking care to place a bundle beside her, before pitching forward onto the grass. It was only as they reached her that Gabe noticed that everything she wore was saturated with water and that she'd wrapped her head in a man's tunic. Looking at it, he realized it was the same as the ones that Dan, Hal and the other soldiers had been wearing. How had she gotten hold of it?

Gabe had a bad feeling there was a soldier lying in the woods with a very sore head right now.

"Water!" Midge said, breaking into his reverie. "She needs water."

Scarlett disappeared through the bushes to the small stream that ran to one side of the thicket, reappearing with a bucket of water and a dipper.

Merry carefully unwrapped the tunic that covered her sister's face and held her head, pouring water into the side of Gwyn's unresponsive mouth.

"Gwyn!" she said. "Gwynnie, wake up!"

"Put her on her side," said Gabe. "It will be easier for her to breathe."

Merry stared at him. "How do you know?" she asked, easing Gwyn onto her side as she spoke. Albert flew down to perch quietly on Midge's shoulder, seeming to peer as anxiously at Gwyn's still form as the others.

"Six months in the Infirmarium," said Gabe, his attention on Gwyn. "I learned a lot, but it wasn't really for me."

"Why not?" asked Merry and Gabe sensed she wasn't really interested but was trying to distract the others.

"Too much blood," he said with a grimace. "And leeches. Too many leeches."

Scarlett shuddered. "Sounds awful," she said.

"Oh, it was," said Gabe, keeping a close eye on Gwyn. He could see her eyelids beginning to flutter and a surge of relief went through him, even as he felt the first raindrops on his head.

"I liked the herbs and seeing how they worked, but there was too much pus and blood for me."

Gwyn coughed and suddenly retched, vomiting black-tinged liquid all over the grass. "How about vomit?" she said, weakly. "How do you feel about that?"

Gabe laughed. "I don't think I've ever been so happy to see vomit in my life," he said, realizing it was true. The strange, prickly girl might rib him mercilessly, but she had proved a loyal friend even though she barely knew him.

Wincing and coughing, Gwyn sat up, looking around her. "Where is it?" she asked, anxiously.

Gabe moved quickly to one side, grabbing the bundle that had been forgotten as they'd all huddled around Gwyn. "It's here!" he said, handing it to her and managing a smile as she hugged it close.

"I got it," she said to Merry, tears in her eyes. "Every last piece."

Merry tried to laugh, as the rain began to tumble down in earnest. "Oh Gwyn," she said. "You shouldn't have – you know you shouldn't."

"How could I not?" was all Gwyn said, raising her face to the cleansing rain and waving a hand in the direction of the still-burning oak. Gabe stared at it sadly, knowing that the cipher was either burnt to a cinder or so smoke-damaged as to be useless.

"Albert says thank you," Midge said solemnly, reminding Gabe that Gwyn had been so close to the book . . . He shook his head at the thought. Much better that Gwyn focus on saving the living, breathing Albert for Midge, who'd already lost so much, rather than a dusty old manuscript.

"Albert's very welcome," said Gwyn. "Though he wasn't too happy when I pulled that hood off him . . . I swear that bird hates me."

Midge smiled. "Not anymore."

"Come on," said Eddie. "If Gwyn can move, we should do so. Those soldiers will be back – or at the very least be heading to Rothwell full of stories about the madman who stepped through a door in a burning tree."

Scarlett giggled. "If they tell it like that, they're the ones who'll be branded madmen," she said.

"Perhaps," said Eddie, soberly, "but it's just crazy enough to bring Ronan of Feldham here to investigate."

"I'm okay," Gwyn said, weakly, trying to stand. Merry gently took the bundle from her as she helped Gwyn to her feet.

"We'll go back to the horses," Merry said. "We'll be safe enough there for tonight and we can decide what to do tomorrow."

Still staring at the tree, rain running into his eyes, Gabe nodded, though his heart ached. What would they do tomorrow? He'd lost the cipher, Eddie had no way to prove the boy wearing his crown was an imposter, and none of them had a home.

"Come on, Gabe," said Eddie, putting an arm around Gabe's shoulder. "We'll figure something out. Maybe the rain will put the fire out before it reaches the book."

"The book!" croaked Gwyn, putting her hand to her forehead in alarm. "I'm sorry, Sandals, I forgot to tell you – I moved the book."

Startled, Gabe swung around to look at her. "You what?" he whispered.

"I moved it," she said. "When I came back for your robe before we went to pull you out of the Abbey, I took the book with me. I wasn't sure if we'd need it for . . . negotiations at any point."

Eddie threw a pointed look at Gabe but said nothing.

"So," Gabe said, licking lips that were dry, despite the rain, "where did you put it?"

"Remember the tall white oak, at the fork in the main path?" she asked, and he noticed now that her eyes were twinkling. "It's there, safely tucked away out of the rain in an old woodpecker nest about halfway up."

Unable to stop himself, Gabe threw his arms around Gwyn. "Whoa!" she said, taking a step back. "Take a tip from Albert. Gratitude from a distance is fine."

Gabe laughed, suddenly feeling lighter than he had since Brother Benedict had handed him the book. He took a big step back, feeling the rain puddling down into his boots, and said with mock formality: "Distant thank you."

Gwyn stepped forward and punched him in the arm: "Close you're welcome," she said and they all dissolved into laughter.

CHAPTER TWELVE

"It's very beautiful," said Midge, holding the cipher reverently in both hands and turning it over in the firelight. Opening the first page, she gasped in wonder at the tree illustration.

"It's one of the most amazing books I've ever seen," Gabe admitted, peering over her shoulder as the gold on the tiny bird flashed and winked.

"You're so lucky," she said, turning to another page. "I've never held a book before and you've seen so many."

"Doesn't seem to have taught him his knee from his elbow when it comes to daily living," said Gwyn from the other side of the small fireplace. The horses whickered softly at the other end of the stable building as Scarlett brushed down Jasper – giving Borlan a wide berth, Gabe noticed.

"Oh hush," said Merry now. "Gabe's done all right. If it weren't for him, Eddie would be buried in a dungeon at Rothwell Castle – or worse."

"Like Pa, you mean," said Gwyn, staring into the fire. She'd managed the journey back from the oak tree in the rain but, Gabe had soon discovered, at the cost of a raging fever.

Merry had dried her off, dressed her warmly in Gabe's robes, and then sat on her until she'd promised to lie down quietly and rest. While all that was going on, Gabe and Midge had searched the farm's herb garden for feverfew, which Gabe had brewed into a tea.

Despite her protests that she was fine, Gabe noticed that Gwyn had sipped the tea slowly but surely until it was gone, and then fallen into a deep sleep. She'd woken a short time ago, and Gabe was relieved to note that her normal level of feistiness was returning.

"We'll get Pa out," Merry said, holding her sister's hand. "Winterfest is still eight weeks away." Gabe looked away. This year, summer seemed endless, but autumn had officially begun weeks ago.

"We don't even know where he is," Gwyn said, bitterly. "And he's sick. How long will he survive?"

Merry said nothing, and Gabe swallowed hard, knowing that Gwyn's words were true. Particularly if Lord Sherborne now knew who the girls were and that they were keeping company with him and Eddie.

"Oh!" Midge gasped, drawing Gabe's attention back to the book. "Oh, Gabe, look!"

Gabe frowned. Midge didn't have the book open to a page, rather she was holding it closed, with the gilt edge towards him. "Watch," she said, slipping the leather cover back a tiny bit so that the gilt-edged pages were slightly fanned. As she did so, Gabe watched openmouthed as a beautiful scene appeared on the side of the book.

"And then it disappears," she said, pushing the cover back into position. The dull gold of the gilt pages reflected nothing.

"May I see?" Gabe said, and she handed him the book. He fanned the pages and looked closely at the hand-painted scene. A deep-green sea of trees began at the outer edges of the pages, rising up into the center to show a snow-topped peak. Squinting in the firelight, Gabe could make out a tiny castle of some sort, perched on the left side of the mountain, looking as though it would slide down at any moment.

"What is it?" asked Eddie, striding over for a closer look and standing over Gabe's shoulder.

"It's called fore-edge painting," Gabe said. "I've heard about it, but I've never seen it before. It's a specialist craft, known only to a few."

Gabe handed it up to Eddie, his mind working furiously. What was the painting? Was it just another code that made no sense? He couldn't help but wonder why Brother Benedict had wanted *this* book saved. Perhaps they should let it fall into Lord Sherborne's hand and it could drive *him* mad as he tried to unearth its secrets.

"Oh!" said Eddie. "I know this place."

"You do?" said Gabe, leaping to his feet. "Where is it?"

"I've never been there," Eddie said, "but I've seen a painting of this place. It's the home of Sir Lucien Thergood, formerly Brother Lucien."

There was a silence.

"You're sure his name is Lucien?" asked Gabe.

"Oh yes," said Eddie, cheerfully. "He'd be ancient now if he's still alive, but he used to be my grandfather's most trusted advisor. He and my father had a falling out years ago."

"What about?" asked Merry.

"Nobody knows," said Eddie. "My father never spoke of it again, but Lucien stormed from the castle one night leaving all his belongings behind in his chamber at court."

"But you saw the painting?" Gabe asked.

"Yes," said Eddie, staring at the edge of the book. "My father keeps it in his solar." Eddie stopped, looking up. "I never thought to ask why," he said, "but now that I think of it . . . I wonder why he keeps it so close."

Gabe barely heard, still unable to swallow his disappointment that this was not the key he was seeking to unlocking the mystery of Aidan.

"Where is it?" asked Midge, as Eddie handed the book back to her.

Eddie sighed. "It's about as far north as you can go and still be in Alban," he said. "Lucien really wanted to put distance between himself and my father. It's up near the border with Caledon."

Merry laughed. "I don't even know where that is," she said. "We've never been outside the forest."

"It's a long way," Eddie said with a smile. "At least three weeks' journey on horseback, if not longer. And then it's up a mountain, almost in the clouds by the looks of the painting that I saw."

"What's it called, this castle in the clouds?" asked Gwyn.

Gabe could almost see her strength returning – and with it her restlessness. He wondered what she would do the following day, when they'd still be hiding out in this stable while Lord Sherborne and Prior Dismas combed the countryside for them.

"Oh, gadzooks, now you're testing me," said Eddie, scratching his head. "I think it's . . . yes . . . it's Hayden's Mont." The last words came out in such a triumphant rush that Gabe nearly missed them.

"Did you say 'Hayden's Mont'?" he asked, almost unable to breathe.

Gwyn sat up straighter and Gabe knew she remembered Malachy's note.

"Yes, that's it," said Eddie, nodding furiously. "I'm sure it is!"

Gwyn whooped with delight, her voice cracking at the high note. "Aidan!" she said. "It wasn't Aidan, it was Hayden!"

Eddie looked confused. "I wish I had some idea what you're talking about," he said.

"Eddie, you've just solved a huge mystery!" said Gabe, almost dancing with delight. "I have to take the book to *Hayden's Mont*. I know where to go."

Eddie frowned. "Maybe," he said. "But it's the other side of the kingdom, Gabe. How are you going to get there on your own?"

Gabe stilled, realizing the magnitude of the task ahead.

"He won't be alone," came Merry's decisive voice. "We'll be with him."

"What?" shrieked Scarlett, giving the horses a fright. "We'll what?"

"Well, you can stay to be captured by Lord Sherborne and handed back to your father if you want," said Merry, "but Gwyn, Midge and I will go with Gabe. We need to lie low for at least the next few weeks and what better way than to leave the forest completely? Lord Sherborne will never think to look for us outside the confines of the three local villages."

Eddie cleared his throat, but Merry kept talking. "As for you, Eddie, you're not safe here while that imposter wears your crown. And we need you in that crown to save our pa."

"I could head home," Eddie said, "tell my father what's happened."

"You could," said Gwyn, "but you will arrive at the palace in rags, spouting a story about being the Prince when everyone knows the Prince is attending tournaments in Rothwell, and you will be thrown into a dungeon before you get anywhere near the King."

Merry shook her head sadly. "She's right, Eddie. We have to find another way to get your throne back, and maybe this Lucien is the key?"

Eddie hesitated.

"Besides," Merry went on, "you're the only one who knows where Hayden's Mont is – are you going to repay Gabe's bravery at the tournament by abandoning him now?"

Eddie sighed. "All right then," he conceded. "Given I can't see another solution at present, I'll come. With any luck that imposter will make a mistake and give himself away in the next few months."

Gabe shook his head. "I've been thinking about that," he said. "I think he's been drugged. Did you see how slow and blank he was at the tournament? He won't be allowed to make a mistake."

"All the more reason to find Lucien then," said Merry, firmly. "The five of us will leave tomorrow."

"And Albert," said Midge, nodding towards the door. "The five of us, and Albert."

Albert had been tethered safely in a nearby tree – Eddie had suggested bringing him inside, recognizing the bird for the valuable creature that he was, but the girls had laughed.

"Spoken like a boy who has servants," Merry had said. "If you'd ever cleaned up the floor under a tethered falcon, particularly one who's been allowed to hunt all the way here, you wouldn't even consider bringing him inside."

"Um," came a small voice near the horses now, "if you're all going, I'd like to come too, if you don't mind."

Merry laughed with relief. "I hoped you'd say that, cousin," she said, pulling Scarlett into the circle in front of the fire. "I'd get awfully lonely on Jasper without you."

Merry turned back to the others. "With the horses, it won't take as long to get there," she said. "And then we can get back here to rescue Pa and topple the imposter."

Later, as the others settled down to sleep in front of the fire, excited about the journey they would begin the next day, Gabe carefully wrapped the book in the oiled cloth before placing it under his head to sleep on. He had decided that he would not let the book out of his sight ever again, and Scarlett had offered to stitch him a small pouch from the oiled cloth at the first opportunity so that he could wear it slung across his chest – or under his clothing.

After much thought, he'd decided to stay in his breeches and tunic, though Gwyn had insisted that they pack his Abbey robes in the small bundle of goods they were planning to take with them. Merry had taken her mother's crockery and hidden it in the farm's woodshed, but Gwyn had also insisted on taking one precious teacup with them, arguing that it was important to keep their parents with them in some form or other.

Gabe could scarcely believe that they were all about to undertake a long and no-doubt arduous journey into the unknown, just to help him. It was hard to imagine that only days ago he'd been tucked up in the dormitory at the Abbey, surrounded by the loud snoring of postulants and novices. Now, all he could hear was the slow, steady breathing of his friends and the occasional snort from the horses.

Gabe was glad that he and his new friends were all safe and warm, though he shuddered to think of the dangers they'd faced during their days together so far. He could only hope that Brother Malachy had managed to save the Abbot from the dungeon and that the worst was behind them all.

He thought about the questions that now had answers – the whereabouts of the Abbot, the identity of the mysterious Aidan, the truth of Eddie's claim – but he also considered the many, many new questions that had been uncovered, questions that he couldn't imagine ever having answers to.

And at the heart of it all was the book. For so long, it had been a book of secrets. Prior Dismas had called it the Ateban Cipher, but in Gabe's mind it was now simply a book of questions.

ACKNOWLEDGEMENTS

I have enjoyed beyond belief the opportunity to unlock the secrets of new worlds and characters with Gabe, Merry, Gwyn, Scarlett, Midge and Eddie, but it's so much easier to do so when you have a stable team around you.

Thank you to Jo Butler and the team at Cameron's for guiding the journey, and to the intrepid team at Hachette Australia, particularly Suzanne O'Sullivan, Kate Stevens, Tom Bailey-Smith, Chris Kunz, Ashleigh Barton, Fiona Hazard, Justin Ractliffe and Louise Sherwin-Stark, as well as ANZ cover designers Blacksheep and illustrator Paul Young.

Thank you to my extended family with love and to my friends (you know who you are) who continue to keep my feet on the ground while my head remains firmly in the clouds.

A special thank you to my first readers Sophie, Jody, Anna, Georgia, Lilly, Joe and Lucas, who took Gabe and his friends to heart from the opening lines and encouraged me all the way.

And, as always, all my love to my boys: John, Joseph and Lucas. Every book is for you.